GRANDMA VS HITLER

DEREK E. MILLER

LJ EMORY
PUBLISHING

Cover & Layout Copyright © 2019 by L. J. Emory Publishing

Cover & Interior design by Jacob Miller, L. J. Emory Publishing

Published by L. J. Emory Publishing

For information about special discounts for bulk purchases, please contact L. J. Emory Publishing, sales@ljemorypublishing.com

ISBN: 978-1-940283-48-7

ISBN: 978-1-940283-49-4 (eBook)

ONE

SEVENTEEN-YEAR-OLD OWEN PETROV heard his dad's busted muffler long before he saw him drive into the entrance of the school parking lot. This was not good. Apparently, his dad had chosen yet again to drive the old blue Oldsmobile—the rust bucket that refused to die—to pick him up from basketball practice.

He stared in the opposite direction. Didn't his dad realize that maintaining a level of cool at Richmond Falls High School was hard enough without being seen in a vehicle that should have been put out of its misery years ago?

If only Dad had driven Mom's new silver Camry with the sunroof and working muffler, that would have been okay. Nothing embarrassing about the silver Camry.

What Owen did not see, nor did his dad, was the dark green Ford Mustang running the stop sign that so many of the school teenagers routinely blew past. Normally a policemen would be parked there but not today. He heard a scream—some girl on the sidewalk who saw what was about to happen—and the scream made him look up, just as the Mustang plowed into the driver's side of his dad's Oldsmobile.

Metal crunched, glass shattered, and tires squealed. As Owen ran toward the two wrecked cars, he felt like he was in the middle of one of those dreams when time slowed down and trying to run was like forcing his legs through molasses.

Ms. Thompson, a teacher, was outside the school and also saw the accident unfold. He heard her calling 911 as he reached his father's crumpled car.

His dad was unconscious, and blood seemed to be everywhere. Owen tried to wrench the car door open, but it was stuck and no amount of tugging was going to get it open.

Wrecked cars exploded, didn't they?

"Somebody help me!" he shouted. "I gotta get him out of there!"

Two of his friends tried to help, but no matter how much muscle they put into it, they could not get the door open. His father was unconscious but breathing. He prayed that the ambulance would arrive soon. There was hope if they could just get him out.

The other driver punched her way out from behind the deployed airbag, climbed out of the car, sat down on the curb, and burst into tears. The school was large, and Owen did not know her. She was uninjured except for a beet red face from getting hit by the airbag.

Some would say they were just doing their job, and some would say the firemen were heroic. To Owen they seemed like angels sent straight from heaven as they used the Jaws of Life to free his father. Moments later a helicopter landed in the middle of the road. Seconds after that, his dad was loaded into the chopper. It rose into the air, then as fast as it could fly, it took his dad to the Cleveland Clinic. They did not allow him to ride with his dad since he was a minor.

Owen knew he was in shock but didn't realize how bad until he had to stop and think for several seconds before he could remember his mom's phone number when Ms. Thompson asked.

She contacted his mom. Then she steered him toward her car and drove the twenty miles to the Cleveland Clinic. He vaguely remembered her trying to talk to him, but he was fairly certain he did not respond. His brain wasn't working particularly well. He was still trying to process everything that had happened.

He still wished his dad had been driving the Camry. Not because it was newer and better-looking now, but because it had a better safety rating. If his dad had been driving the Camry, there was a chance the impact wouldn't have done so much damage.

It seemed a lifetime ago that he'd been upset that his dad was driving a car he was ashamed to be seen in. The only thing that mattered to him right now was getting to his father as fast possible.

His dad was annoying and often times embarrassing. Sometimes he would deliberately act goofy or tell horrible dad jokes, just to tease Owen in front of his friends. Of all things that popped in Owen's head was his last dad joke at basketball practice. "What do you call fake pasta? An Impasta!" His friends roared with laughter at that one.

His dad really got on his nerves when he bugged him to get off his phone or the computer, or to turn off his video games, and study.

But his dad also came to every basketball game and cheered like a crazy man when Owen made a basket. When he had a bad game and didn't score any points at all, his dad didn't yell at him like some of the other fathers. He just slung an arm around Owen's shoulders, told him he'd do better next time, and took him home to lick his wounds in private. Then, about a half hour later, his dad would show up with an extra-large pizza and cokes, and they'd watch old *Star Trek* reruns together until he started feeling better.

Thinking about his dad coming home with pizza to make him feel better after he'd screwed up a game brought tears to his eyes and sobs up from his chest—and no matter how hard he tried to be a man and stop crying, he couldn't do it.

He'd never cared much for Ms. Thompson as a teacher, but he never forgot her kindness in saying absolutely nothing to try to make things better. She kept her eyes on the road, drove as fast as she legally could, and when she stopped for a traffic light, she reached into the back seat, grabbed a box of Kleenex for him, and kept going.

The drive to the Cleveland Clinic, which normally took a half hour, took Ms. Thompson just over an hour. The traffic was terrible. A torrential rain had come out of nowhere. Cars were pulled over on both sides of the highway waiting for the weather to clear. At one point, they hit a stretch of surface-water and spun out of control, but Ms. Thompson fought the wheel and managed to stabilize the car.

Owen found himself impressed, despite his worry about his dad.

"My dad was a professional race-car driver," she explained, when things were back to normal again. "He made sure I knew how to handle a vehicle."

When they arrived at the hospital, the teacher let him off at the front of the emergency entrance and then went to find a parking place.

Owen saw his mother in the waiting room and ran to her. There was anguish in her eyes when she looked up at him. Her cheeks were wet with tears. She was rubbing her hands together, a habit she reverted to when she was extremely nervous.

Owen sat down and put his arm around her shoulder. "Have you heard anything? How is he?"

"Honey, all I know is they rushed him into surgery. No one's given me any new information."

Until this moment, it had always seemed as though this sort of thing only happened to people on TV.

Ms. Thompson came in from parking her car and sat on the other side of Owen's mom. His teacher and his mom knew each other from a book club they were in. His mother hung onto Ms. Thompson's hand on one side and his hand on the other. No one had anything to say. There was nothing to say. All they could do was wait.

After what seemed like forever, a tall, pale scruffy-faced doctor came through the swinging doors.

"Are you Mrs. Petrov?" he asked.

"Yes."

"I'm Dr. Cramer. We just finished the surgery. Your husband had a crushed leg, two broken ribs, and some internal bleeding. The bleeding was bad, but we got it stopped, and he's stable now. He'll be in intensive care for a few days, but with any luck, he should be okay eventually. It's going to be a long healing process, though."

Owen heard his mother let out a deep breath, as though she'd been holding it in for a long time. Then she jumped up, grabbed the doctor, and hugged him.

"Thank you, doctor," she said. "Thank you so much!"

"Mom?" Owen was a little embarrassed by watching his mother hug a stranger.

"It's okay, son," the doctor said. "I like getting hugged a lot better than getting yelled at."

"Can we go see him?" Owen asked.

"Give us a few minutes to get him set up in ICU. A nurse will come get you when you can go in. I'm going to go try to get some sleep now. It's been a long day and night here in the ER. Weather like this brings a lot of bad stuff in."

With that last comment, the doctor went back through the doors.

"Alexei's going to be okay." His mom collapsed into the chair, held her hands in the air, and said, "Thank you, Jesus!"

Owen glanced at Ms. Thompson. Sometimes his mom could be a bit too religious for his comfort. Then his teacher added a hearty "Amen!" and he relaxed. Truth be told, he had been praying nearly nonstop ever since he saw the wreck.

He sat down next to his mom and put his arm back around her.

"You're shaking," his mom said.

"I know. I can't seem to stop."

"I understand," she said, patting his knee. "You came within minutes of having to be the man of the house."

"Would you like for me to go get your mother-in-law and bring her here?" Ms. Thompson asked.

"Oh, would you? I know she'd want to be here. Alexei's her only child."

"No problem at all," Ms. Thompson said. "Just call her and let her know I'm on my way. I'm afraid she'll be so upset I might not be able to communicate with her too well."

"Her English does get a bit iffy when she's under stress," his mom said, writing down his grandmother's address and handing it to the teacher.

As his teacher left to go get his grandmother, a nurse came out.

"Mrs. Petrov, if you come with me, I'll take you and your son in to see your husband. He's not yet awake, but you can sit with him if you like. Sometimes it's comforting for a patient to see a loved one the first thing when they wake up."

It was a different experience for Owen, sitting with his mother on one side of his father's hospital bed. He listened to the machines clicking on and off. He listened to the hiss of his father's breath coming in and out. It wasn't really his father's breath. It was a machine that was doing the breathing, keeping him alive.

Owen grew up a bit while they waited for his father to awaken and for his grandmother to arrive. He had so many good memories of his dad, and he realized that he desperately wanted to make more.

He didn't know what to expect when his grandmother got there. He hoped she wouldn't fall apart. It was all he could do to be strong for his mother, let alone deal with a hysterical Russian grandmother. Or worse. His grandmother was so old. Seeing her only son lying there bruised and battered and on a breathing machine might just kill her.

Well, at least they would be in the right place. There would be staff here to care for her if she fainted or became hysterical or —God forbid—had a heart attack.

When his grandmother did come into the hospital room, she did none of these things. Instead, she walked right over to the bed, stared at her son, and made a small clucking sound in the back of her throat before she bent over and kissed his forehead.

"I am here now," she said. "I will see that the doctors do the right things. You will get better, Alexei, I promise."

Then she took off her gloves and stuffed them into the pocket of her coat, removed the grey head scarf she had tied beneath her chin, unbuttoned her long coat, took the heavy black purse off her arm, and handed the whole bundle to Owen.

"Here," she said. "Make yourself useful. Please hang this up."

Owen was actually grateful to feel useful for a few moments as he helped his grandmother.

"Thank you for coming, Klara," his mom said.

"Thank you for sending your friend to come for me, although

I would have walked to be with my son if that was the only way."

"In this weather?" Owen asked, incredulously. His grandmother's assisted living apartment was over a mile away.

"I would have walked," Grandmother insisted. "Is not so far. For my Alexei, I would crawl if it was the only way to get to him. Tell me what happened."

After hearing the basics of the wreck, she grew silent. His grandmother, usually full of laughter, was not talkative tonight. Instead she took a long hard look at her daughter-in-law. "You do not look so good. You should go home and rest."

"I don't want to leave Alexei."

"It is silly for both of us to be here right now. You worked all day and should go home."

"You need your rest, too," his mother said.

"I am an old woman," the grandmother said. "I need less sleep. I will stay."

"I'm not leaving the hospital."

"Then go lie on a couch in the waiting room. Owen, be a good boy and go watch over your mother."

He knew better than to disobey his grandmother. If there was one thing his father insisted on, it was that he treat his mother and grandmother with respect. His mother did look weary.

"As long as he is stable," she said, "I think I will go close my eyes. Thank you, Klara."

He accompanied his mother out to the waiting room. He got her a snack and a drink from the vending machine. Then he folded up his jacket to make a pillow for her as she curled up on a small couch.

For a while, he tried to read a magazine, but it was about medical things, and he didn't want to think about medical things right now. Then, he decided to check on his grandmother and father yet again. When he peeked in, his grandmother was holding his father's hand, rocking back and forth, singing something he remembered from his childhood when he would sometimes stay over at her house. It was a Russian lullaby, with words he did not understand.

Quietly, he closed the door and went back to the waiting room. Watching his grandmother grieve over her son made his throat close up, and tears come to his eyes.

Life was so much simpler when all he had to worry about was school work and playing video games.

For the next few days, Owen, his mother, and grandmother took turns staying in his father's hospital room. Finally his father was taken off the breathing machine, but it took a while for the painkillers and shock of the accident to fade a bit. It took a while before his father could even remember what day it was.

After the second week in the hospital, the doctor released him to go home. A physical therapist and home nurse were to come work with him twice a week.

Owen's dad was weak, but so grateful to be going home. "What day is it again?"

When Owen told him the date, his dad turned to Grandmother, speaking in Russian. He seemed agitated about something; his grandmother's voice was soothing.

Grandmother had tried to teach Owen her language many times, but he hadn't been all that interested. Now he could only make out a couple words: "friends" and "last time."

His grandmother kept shaking her head no, like it didn't matter.

Finally, Owen's dad turned to him and said, "You know I was going to take your grandmother to Russia for a visit in a few weeks?"

Owen had a vague recollection that something like that was going to happen. He hadn't paid much attention to it.

"It is her 60th reunion and possibly the last one she and her friends will ever have. She says it is not that important to go, but I know it is. Would you be willing to take her in my place?"

"Me?" His head spun at the mere thought. "Take Grandmother to Russia? By myself?"

He wanted to add *but I'm just a kid! I can't do that.* But he knew that would sound wimpy. Actually, he knew even the fact he was hesitating was wimpy.

"Owen, the other choice is for me to take Klara," his mother said. "But you would have to stay home from school and take care of your dad."

Really? He could skip school and play video games and just hang out with his father? That didn't sound too bad.

His dad had always had an uncanny way of reading his mind.

"You also will get to cook my meals, change my bandages, cater to my every demand, and help me sit on the toilet," his dad said. "I will probably need some sponge baths as well."

Owen gave it some thought.

"Dad," he said, "I would seriously rather face the Russian Red Army than give you a sponge bath."

"That's my boy!" his father said. "Now, is there a wheelchair in this place? I want to go home!"

Inwardly, Owen groaned. This really was a no-win situation. What young man wanted to take his 78-year-old grandmother to Russia? It was April, and it was probably still frozen over there, for all he knew. When he thought of Russia, he imagined nothing but gray buildings and snow. In fact, considering that he was just one generation from living there, he knew very little about the country at all.

TWO

THE NEXT COUPLE of weeks were crazy. A passport and last-minute travel visa to Russia had to be secured for him. School was still in session, but the principal was able to excuse him, as long as he came back and gave a report to his class about the experience.

To his credit, Owen started reading everything he could on Russia. As he read, he discovered that it was a massive country and had much more interesting history than he'd known.

He also began to realize that although he saw his grandmother on an almost weekly basis, he didn't know all that much about her past, other than she had come from Moscow and had taught the Russian language at a small nearby community college. Even though widowed now and retired, she still tutored many of the Russian language students there.

His grandfather had passed away before he was born. His

grandmother and grandfather had immigrated to the United States. Owen's dad had been born in Cleveland. His grandmother had made sure her son was fluent in Russian, but for some reason, learning the Russian language had never appealed to Owen.

As he packed, his father cautioned him to pack light, so that he could also carry his grandmother's stuff. Thankfully, his father was improving daily, so Owen wasn't too worried about leaving his parents behind for those two weeks.

Finally, the big day to leave had come. His mother drove them to the airport. They would be on a connecting flight in Los Angeles, where they would switch planes to Moscow.

Owen tried to be very patient with his grandmother as he helped her go through security. He made sure she was settled into her window seat before fastening his own seatbelt in the dreaded middle seat. She gave him a big smile in the reflection of the window as the engines kicked in for takeoff.

"You did not want to do this." She nodded. "No, don't pretend. I know it is a sacrifice. But I thank you for coming anyway. It is something I could have done alone. I am not yet so old that I need a babysitter, but it is always better to travel with someone you love. Then you get to enjoy it two times. Once for yourself and once for the one you care about. This trip will be good for both of us. You need to see my country, and so do I."

THREE

Helping grandmother make the connecting flight was not as big a deal as he thought. The airline made sure there was someone with an electric cart that whisked them from gate to gate. Grandmother smiled when they were going fast, threw her hands up as they went around one corner, and said, "Wheeeeee!"

He laughed with her. He had never heard her make that sound of glee before. It seemed she really enjoyed the air rushing by them.

They were dropped off at the next plane that would take them into Moscow. Again, he made sure they both were buckled in for takeoff.

This part of the flight he knew would be miserable. It was going to be a long, boring, direct flight. But he cheered up when he thought about the fact that at least he was missing out on Mrs. Peters' civics class. Now that was boring!

He made the best he could of the trip, getting up and walking around from time to time to keep from getting "numb butt". He made sure his grandmother got up and walked a little as well. It seemed each time he helped her out of her seat it got easier. It was as though the closer they got to Russia, the more alive she became.

Owen had watched all the TV and movies he could stand already on the plane's entertainment system. His grandmother didn't bother with any of that. Instead, she kept pulling out an old, tattered, leather book. Owen could tell that it was hand-written. There were old photographs stuffed in the pages here and there. She would pull one out from time to time and smile.

Owen wondered vaguely what kind of reunion she was going to. He assumed it was the Russian equivalent of a high school reunion. His grandmother was 78. If this was her 60th reunion, then the math worked out. She would have been 18 years old 60 years earlier. He couldn't think of any kind of reunion that could happen for an eighteen-year-old except high school graduation.

A few more hours passed; then all the lights came on in the cabin, and an announcement was made. First it was in Russian. Owen's grandmother just shook her head in a *tsk tsk tsk* fashion. Then the announcement was made in English.

There was a problem with the plane, and to be safe, they

would land at the first airport that could handle the size of their airplane. This was a worry. How was he supposed to take care of his grandmother if the plane let them off in the middle of nowhere in Russia?

FOUR

THE PLANE LANDED JUST FINE, which was the good news. The bad news was the plane would not be taking off again for a few days, and there was no plane to come pick them up. Owen's fear of being stuck in Russia with his elderly grandmother was coming true.

Soon they were standing in the middle of the airport terminal. The airline was trying to find hotels for everyone and from the looks on the people's faces around him, he got the impression they were not having much luck.

They were in Irkutsk, Russia. He wasn't sure if he was pronouncing it right, but at least he was able to text on what little battery he had left on his cell phone to tell his parents what had happened so far.

Then his grandmother said, "This way. Come on."

Owen followed her. She found someone who looked like they worked there and talked to them a mile a minute.

Then she turned to him. "Please go get the bags, Owen."

She pointed to where the airline had started to unload their luggage. Owen did as he was told and wondered where they were going to go with their luggage.

He returned to his grandmother, and she said, "Follow me."

Owen followed close behind. He had no idea where they were going, nor could he understand a word of the language people were using all around him. She didn't really need his help in any way that he could see, except for carrying their luggage.

Now that they were on Russian soil, she was clearly taking command of the situation, while he, the grandson who was supposed to be taking care of her, felt like a tag-along.

Outside was a black small old car that was not western manufactured. Owen helped the driver load their luggage as his grandmother got into the car. Once Owen was in the car he figured he might as well practice a little and asked her in what little Russian he knew.

"Where go?"

"Good!" She smiled encouragingly. "Practice that Russian! You are going to need it. We are going on a train."

About fifteen minutes later, the car dropped them off at the train station. He could recognize some of the other passengers from the plane who also had the same idea. His grandmother walked to the train ticket counter and purchased two train tickets.

"They say the train will be here in thirty minutes," she said.

"That soon!" He felt very relieved. "That's great."

Then he realized she was watching him with a mischievous grin.

"Here is a language lesson," she said. "In Russian that translates to maybe in an hour and a half. Trains are always late in Russia."

She was right. He was grateful when it finally pulled into the station two hours later.

They boarded the train and once again started on their journey to Moscow. He was excited to discover that they were riding on the train referred to as the Trans-Siberian Express. It was a famous train route he had seen mentioned in movies a couple of times. He made lots of mental notes of what the train looked like, hoping he could use the details for part of his presentation when he got back to school.

It was going to take about four days to get there, so his grandmother told him he should get comfortable. They had, at her insistence, built an extra four days into the schedule as a cushion, in case something went wrong. Now he was grateful at her planning. Even after all this time, she knew her country and had purposely added extra time to make certain they wouldn't come all this way and miss her reunion.

His grandmother must have spent extra on the tickets, because they seemed to be in one of the best cars. The seats laid back further than the airplane seats, so he was a lot more comfortable.

Although his grandmother had taken charge like a much younger person, once they were on the train, her age started catching up with her. When they started moving, she drifted off to sleep like she had ridden in trains all her life.

Owen couldn't sleep. His sleep schedule was completely messed up. He walked up and down the aisles and various other train cars until he had the train memorized. Then he went back to his seat. Grandmother was still asleep. There was nothing to do except stare out the window of the train. Although he was in a foreign country, even that got tiring after a while. There was no reading material in English on the train. Nothing to do.

He finally glanced down. With the corner sticking out of her carry-on bag, he saw her old leather book she had been reading. He was curious but knew it would not be right to just grab it.

She woke up about then, looked at him and smiled. "You ask no questions of your Russian grandmother, but I see many questions in your eyes. I am no longer tired. I would not mind talking with my smart grandson."

"Okay," he said. "What was it like living here?"

She thought a moment. "Life was very hard, but we made the best of it. It helped that I did not know any better, and my parents were kind and gentle. They sheltered me from most of the hardships of my youth. I did not know they were hardships until I moved to America."

"I guess if all you know is one thing, you don't know what you're missing," he said. "Sometimes I remind myself not everyone has video games, running water, and stuff like that."

Grandmother laughed. "You should have seen my face the first time your grandfather and I walked into an American grocery store. So much stuff and so many choices. If our pocketbook was not so small that day, we would have bought the whole store."

They continued to talk about details of what her Russian home had been like and what games she played as a young girl in the neighborhood.

That reminded him of something else he'd been wanting to ask.

"What is this reunion we are going to?" he asked. "Is it your high school graduation or something?"

She did not respond, so he thought she had not heard and repeated it.

"I heard you the first time," she said. "I would say it is an Or Something."

"Like what?"

"I have some things in my past that not even your father knows about. Something I struggled with for years trying to decide whether to share it with him. Then this reunion came up. I thought he would come with me, and we could experience it together—just he and I—but now I have you, instead. Somehow I think even a teenager will find it interesting."

Owen was sitting up straight at this point, listening to every word. Grandmother, who always spoke what was on her mind, was being uncharacteristically mysterious.

"Enough time has passed for wounds to have healed in me, and you will see what kind of reunion soon enough, but while you wait…"

Her old hands reached into her bag, and she pulled out the cracked leather book and stared at it. "Other than my wedding ring, this is the most precious earthly possession I own."

She handed the book over to Owen.

"Perhaps it is time for you to learn something from the past. A secret I've held all these years. But I'm not going to make it easy for you. It is written all in Russian. Perhaps you'll learn something as you try to translate it."

He held up his cell phone. "Maybe my learning curve will be shorter than you think. I downloaded a Russian-to-English program on my phone back home."

"Good luck with that," Grandmother chuckled. "Some of my students have attempted to shortchange their lessons by using that device. It did not turn out as well as they hoped. But you go ahead and try. I'm going to take a nap now. We are going to need all our energy once we reach Moscow."

FIVE

As Grandmother slept, Owen found out why she had chuckled when he bragged about his translation program. She knew that fancy electronic translators were not as helpful as he thought. The translating was going much slower than he ever realized. First, he translated the worn title from the leather.

It said, "Diary." No surprise there.

He was about to put the diary back in its place when one of the pictures fell out. He picked it up and blinked when he looked at it. He could not believe what he was seeing. It was a picture of his grandmother in a flight outfit. Her face was dirty, as though she had been sprayed with oil, and she was sitting in an old biplane that had what appeared to be bullet holes in it.

It was probably just a prop from a gag photo. There was no

way his cookie-baking grandmother had ever flown an airplane, let alone one with bullet holes in it.

SIX

IT WAS PAINFUL, trying to read each word and then translate it. He was working on translating some of the writing on the back of that gag photo that had fallen out of the book, when a voice interrupted him.

"Excuse me, are you American?"

He looked up into the prettiest blue eyes he had ever seen.

"Yes," he stammered. "I am."

The girl said, "I thought so. Hi, my name is Nika Rogov." She formally stuck out her hand to shake his.

Owen politely stood and introduced himself, "I'm Owen Petrov, and the woman sleeping here next to me is Klara, my grandmother. How did you guess that I am from America?"

"Your tennis shoes."

"Huh?"

"Americans wear tennis shoes when traveling. Europeans do not."

"I'll remember that next time," he said. "This is the first time I've traveled outside of the U.S.A."

"I've been lucky and traveled a lot, so I have been able to see each countries' little…what is the word I'm looking for…quacks?"

"I think the word you are looking for is *quirks*."

"Yes, quirks, that is the right word."

"You speak English better than some of my friends. Sorry, but I barely speak any Russian. How did you learn it so well?"

"My father is in the oil and gas business, and my mother is American, so she made sure to teach me English. I'm not an expert, but I can get around."

Owen laughed, "I'm afraid that if my grandmother ran away from me here, I would never find my way out of Russia."

"Probably not. Russia is very large. Do you mind if I sit and practice my English with you?"

"Oh, please do; I'm bored out of my mind. We were supposed to be flying, but our plane was grounded. Grandmother managed to get us on this train to Moscow."

"Oh good, I'm going all the way to Moscow as well. Maybe it won't be so boring now that we have met, and you will see some beautiful parts of Russia as we go by. I can be your tour guide and tell you about them."

"That would be great!" Owen was feeling much better. Meeting Nika had definitely made the trip more bearable.

"So, what brings you to Russia?"

"I'm not entirely sure. She's being a bit mysterious about it. My father had planned to take my grandmother to some sort of reunion in Moscow. But he was in an auto accident, and he's still recuperating. I volunteered to accompany my grandmother."

He was glad his grandmother wasn't awake to hear his description of what had happened. He hadn't exactly "volunteered" for anything, but it made him sound manlier than telling her he had come to avoid having to help his dad sit on the toilet.

Nika's dancing eyes grew serious and concerned. "Is your dad going to be ok?"

"Eventually. It could have been much worse. He was in good spirits when I left, though. He was joking about how he was going to make mom peel grapes and feed them to him while I was gone."

Nika giggled. "What did your mother say?"

Giggling girls had always annoyed Owen. But not Nika. She had the cutest giggle he had ever heard.

"Mom told him the only grapes she was going to peel were the ones she planned to throw at him if he got lazy during rehab."

"They sound like they love each other very much."

Owen thought this over. "Yeah, I guess they do." It wasn't something he'd stopped to consider before.

"So, what is this reunion?" Nika asked.

"I really don't know. It is her 60th of whatever. I'm assuming it's her high school graduation. I mean, she would have been 18. What else could it be?"

"When is it?"

"May second."

Nika thought that over. "Our schools don't let out then. It's kind of an odd time to have it."

"Who knows? She gave me her diary and told me to figure it out for myself. It is, of course, in Russian. I think this is her way to punish me for not being more interested in learning her native language. The more mysterious she acts, the more I wish I could break the code."

"Isn't it rude to try to read your grandmother's diary?"

"Normally I would say yes, but she actually gave it to me to read. Probably because she didn't think I could or would do it. Before you came, I was just trying to figure out what was written on this picture that fell out. I'm pretty sure it is of my grandma as a young woman."

He handed the picture to Nika.

Nika's eyes widened. She turned the picture over, scanned the words, and gasped.

"What?" Owen said. "What does it say?"

"It can't be possible," Nika said. "Most of them are dead."

"Most of *who* are dead?"

"The Night Witches."

"The *what?*"

Visions of his grandmother riding a broom materialized.

"A Night Witch! They are greatly revered in Russia. But there are so few left."

SEVEN

"I THINK you might have your English words mixed up. You keep saying, 'night witch.' My grandmother is the furthest thing from a witch."

"I do not have my words mixed up," Nika said. "I know exactly what I am saying."

"My grandmother does not make potions or own a broom that flies. She doesn't own a pointy hat, and she's allergic to cats. Black or otherwise."

"No, no, no. Give me a second to get my words together. The back of the pictures says: *"Me and my trusty PO2 plane after completing our 200th bombing run."*

"Huh?"

"Your grandmother helped save Russia," Nika said, excitedly.

"Actually, I think it is safe to say that your grandmother helped save the world."

"Yeah, right. Helped save the world? Grandmother will have a good laugh when we tell her that one."

"I am no expert, but this is what I know. During World War II, there were three air squadrons of female pilots. One of the squadrons was made up entirely of women. Even the mechanics, weapons people, transportation, fuelers, and pilots. That squadron was the night bombers. They were given the oldest planes—many were from World War I—and some of the planes had been used for crop dusting before the war."

"Again, that's ridiculous. You are talking about my grandmother. She tutors people in Russian and bakes cookies. There is no way she was ever a fighter pilot. Seriously, Nika. That's the wildest thing I've ever heard."

"Perhaps not, but I intend to ask her." Nika continued to study the photo. "The history of the Night Witches is fascinating. I did a research paper for school on it. They only bombed the Germans at night. The woman who created these units, Marina Raskova, was brilliant. She taught these girls to cut the engines of these old outdated planes and silently glide to their targets. The Germans could not hear them coming until they were right over top their heads."

"They were taking a big risk." Owen felt himself being drawn into the story. "What if their engines didn't start again?"

"I know! Right? It was very dangerous, but it worked. The

Germans wouldn't hear anything except a swishing sound. That sound came from the wind passing through the wires between the wings, and they knew the bombs were coming down on their heads right behind that swishing sound. They said it sounded like a witch's broom flying in the night. The squadron didn't name themselves 'Night Witches.' Those women were so hated and feared by the Germans that it was the soldiers themselves who started calling them that. I've heard the women pilots were very proud to have earned that name."

"Sorry," Owen said. "It's a fascinating story, but there's just no way my grandmother was some sort of bomber pilot in World War II."

"There's only one way to find out. Care to join me in the dining car for dinner? Maybe there's something in the diary that will tell us."

"Only if you let me buy and order for me, since I can't read the menu!"

"You are pitiful," she teased. "You should stop being lazy and learn your grandmother's language. I will try not to order anything too weird."

EIGHT

THEY FOUND AN OPEN TABLE, and Nika ordered for them. Then, while they waited, she teased him with all the bizarre things she had ordered. Owen was relieved when the meal arrived to discover that Nika had been kind and only ordered Beef Stroganoff, which was one of his favorite dishes.

"This is Russian food?" he said. "My grandmother makes this at home."

Nika raised an eyebrow. "And that is a surprise?"

He laughed. "I guess it shouldn't be."

This trip was getting better by the minute for Owen. After they had eaten, Nika moved to his side of the table, and sitting close so they could both look at the pages together, she translated the inside cover, "To my darling daughter Klara, may you fill this diary with hopes, dreams, and accomplishments. Love Father."

She stopped reading. "How sweet."

"I guess." He wasn't terribly interested in his grandmother's hopes and dreams. It was the accomplishments he wanted to know about. It wasn't possible that she had been a Night Witch, but his curiosity was definitely piqued.

Nika began reading the first page.

"School will let out soon. Father wants me to record my hopes and dreams. I have many, but with the war going on, I'm not sure the things I hope to do will ever become a reality. Every day bad news comes of the Germans gaining more ground in our Mother Russia. How could they do this to us? We were at peace. We gave them raw materials, and we had a treaty. They attacked us without warning and for no reason."

"Russia was friends with Germany during the war?" Owen asked.

"At the beginning."

"How could they have been friends after what Germany was doing to the Jews?"

"Remember, they didn't have things like the Internet back then. News reporting was spotty. Ordinary Russian citizens did not know what Germany was doing to the innocent civilians caught up in their path."

"I admit, it's easy to forget how quickly information flows now compared to what it was like in the past," Owen said.

"Also, the leaders back then in Russia were pretty oppressive themselves. We had Lenin and Stalin, but that is a conversation for another time. I want to keep digging into this diary."

"Suits me." Owen was curious about his grandmother's diary, but he was also enjoying having a pretty girl sitting close to him.

Nika continued to slowly read aloud. *"I want to join the war effort like the men, but women are turned away. My favorite class is flying. I would really like to fly for the Russian Air Force."*

"Now hang on a second," Owen interrupted. "She took flying classes? While she was in high school?"

"That is something I know nothing about," Nika said. "I can tell you they don't teach flying in high school now. Maybe we can figure that out later."

She continued to read, *"I have the highest marks in flying for my class. I'm even beating the boys, which makes them quite mad. I don't rub it in their faces, but it is fun to see my name at the top of the list that is posted weekly."*

Again, Owen interrupted, "That just blows my mind that flying was taught as a high school class."

"Excuse me," Nika said.

Owen watched as she got up from their table and approached an elderly couple sitting several tables down from them. The man was wearing some medals on his chest. It was strange to see that. He was not in a military uniform.

The old man smiled and spoke with great enthusiasm. The old woman nodded and joined the conversation several times. About ten minutes later, Nika came back to their table.

"What was that all about?" Owen asked.

"He was a World War II veteran. That was his wife. They've been married for fifty-eight years. This is an anniversary trip for them."

"How could you tell for sure that he was a veteran?"

"One thing different here from America is that people who won military medals will wear them long after they are out of the military. They are very proud of them. I noticed that couple the minute we entered the dining car. I asked them if flying was taught in high school when they were young. They were surprised by the question but very pleased to answer. It turns out that Stalin was quite a fan of flying and directed that it be taught in high school. His passion for flying was a lucky thing for Russia, because it gave them a pool of pilots ready for when the war was going on. However, getting enough planes for combat was a big problem. They had a continual shortage of planes."

"Nowadays they won't even let us skateboard at school," Owen said. "I can hardly imagine high school students being allowed to fly as part of their education, but wouldn't that be cool!"

"It would be exciting."

Nika dug back into the diary and continued to read:

"When I fly, I feel so free. The wind blowing in my face, seeing the landscape pass by—it makes you feel like you can do anything."

"Well that explains why she enjoyed driving fast in the airport on the electric cart!"

"I bet!"

Nika turned the page. There had been no entry for several months. Then the diary continued:

"There are rumors that Stalin will start letting females apply to become pilots. All of us in our flying class are trying to find out how to apply once we graduate. Mother and Father would kill me if they knew I was going to volunteer to fight the Germans from a plane. I hear their whispers that the Germans are gaining ground every day. They are trying to make plans to move me out of Moscow to friends who live way east. What they do not realize is that I will not run; I must defend my home, my city, my country!"

Nika stopped reading and said, "It is quite possible that on these very train tracks people were running for their lives from the Germans."

"It is a sobering thought," Owen said. "But I'm still trying to wrap my mind around the fact that my grandmother was willing to take on the German army when she was only a year older than me."

NINE

KLARA AWOKE and stared out the train window.. The countryside of her beloved Russia was rushing by. Mile after mile of simple flat farm land. She saw the houses that were small but she knew were filled with family. There were farm animals out grazing in the pastures.

With Owen gone, probably to explore the rest of the train, she allowed herself to remember. It had been so long since she had seen her homeland. Yes, she loved America and the life she had built there, but it felt good to return to the country where she was born. Where she had become an adult.

She was grateful Owen had found something to occupy himself for a while. Teenage grandsons could not sit still for long, and she was not up to entertaining him much. She was very proud of him, though. He had been treating her with more than his usual patience and kindness on this trip.

Not many young men his age would be willing to travel with an old woman to the other side of the world. She saw much of his grandfather in him. Perhaps it was time to tell him things about his grandfather. Her husband had never given up in anything he did. It reminded her of the determination she'd seen Owen exhibit on the basketball court.

She liked going to his basketball games with her son and daughter-in-law. Owen looked so much like his grandfather. The dark hair, intelligent brown eyes, broad shoulders, and taller than most boys. She especially loved watching the fire in his eyes when he played. He did not give up easily. Some of his unwillingness to give up might have, in part, come from her.

She had been an excellent pilot, but not the very best. Her greatest gift to the war had been her tenacity and her courage under fire. The courage had mainly come from sheer fury. How dare the Germans think they could invade Russia! The thought still made her indignant.

She glanced down at her bag and saw that her precious worn book was missing. At first she was in panic but then remembered giving it to Owen. Perhaps he was reading it right now. She had no idea if this latest translation program he'd downloaded was any good. If it was, then he would be in for a shock. She hoped it was not a mistake to share her secret with him, but perhaps it would be good for him to see her not just as an old woman but as the young woman she once was. The young woman she still was at heart.

Just then she felt a tap on her shoulder. It was Owen, and beside him was a strikingly beautiful girl about his age.

"Ah, I see you found some interesting company on this long trip," Klara said. "Good for you!"

"This is Nika," Owen said. "Nika, this is my Grandmother, Klara Petrov."

"I see you have awakened from your nap," Nika said, kindly. "Would you like some hot tea and cake? We brought it for you."

Grandmother realized that she was very thirsty and a bit hungry. Drinking true Russian tea and eating real Russian cakes would be a delight! How thoughtful of this girl to suggest it.

"Thank you," Klara said in Russian. "I would love some, but please, sit down and tell me about yourself while I eat. It has been so long since I've had a proper Russian conversation!"

Owen felt a little left out as he listened to Nika and Grandmother have what was apparently a delightful conversation between the two women, without understanding more than a handful of words.

Nika suddenly switched to English. "All these years you have had this wonderful grandmother who could have taught you

Russian, and you did not take advantage of it? Shame on you!"

"Yes, shame on you!" Grandmother echoed.

Both women laughed. Nika and Grandmother had only known each other a few minutes and already they were ganging up on him.

Grandmother finished her tea and brushed the leftover crumbs of her cake off her lap. Then she said a few more words in Russian.

Nika immediately stood up. "I'm going to accompany your grandmother to the *tualet*. Then you and I have some homework to do."

"Tualet?" he said.

"Toilet," Grandmother said. "Bathroom. Restroom. Ladies room. You really do need to learn how to communicate, Owen."

When they returned, Nika helped Klara get settled back into her seat.

"Anything else we can do for you, Grandmother?" Owen asked.

Grandmother responded in Russian.

"She said she would like more tea in an hour or two," Nika translated.

So now his grandmother was going to be talking to him only

through Nika? That was fine with him. Nika had the most adorable accent. He could listen to her speak all day.

"No problem, Grandma."

As Nika walked away, Grandmother looked up at Owen and winked, then pointed at his new friend and gave him two thumbs up. Owen was so surprised, he nearly tripped over his own feet.

TEN

"No TIME TO WASTE," Nika said. "Pull out the diary! I can't wait to see what happens next."

"What were you two talking about?" he asked. "I mean that long discussion before you went to the bathroom. Uh, the *tualet*."

"Very good!" Nika beamed. "And it is none of your business. Now, let's continue."

She gently turned pages until she found where they had left off and began reading again.

I sent my letter volunteering my services along with my flying credentials to Marina Raskova. I heard nothing for weeks. Then finally I had enough. Me and several of my girlfriends who were also pilots went to military locations throughout the city, offering our services to go to the front and fight. Everywhere we went we were turned away.

They were only taking women who were nurses or who could support the defense of cities, like antiaircraft gunners. That was not me. I wanted to fly. Not sit on the ground. I ended up at the Air Force headquarters and sat at the guard post all day. Finally, toward evening, a captain who had walked through the guard post several times came out. He stopped and asked why I had been standing in the rain all day.

I told him I was a pilot with hundreds of hours of flight time. I was here to volunteer to fight, and I would not leave until someone talked to me about joining the Air Force. He shook his head in disbelief. I thought it was all over, and I might as well go on home, but it was far from over.

"Come with me," he said. "As luck would have it, Marina Raskova is inside putting together a unit of women pilots. If you're willing to stand in the rain all day, the least I can do is give you a chance to talk to her."

I could not believe my persistence had finally won out.

"Marina is a remarkable woman," he said, as we walked to her office. "Rumor is that she marched into Stalin's office with a box full of letters. She said, 'See all these letters of women volunteering for the front? If you don't let me put together women units, some of them will go there by themselves and get themselves killed!'"

I wondered if my letter was one of the ones that made it into that box.

"She was right," the captain said. "A couple of female pilots ended up stealing a fighter airplane and flew to the front lines to fight. I think that is what finally got Stalin to blink." And with that last word, the captain dropped me off at Marina's office.

I could not believe I had arrived. I walked in, quickly made my introduction, said why I was there, and stated my qualifications.

It also just happens to be my 18th birthday, and today I am a member of the Russian Air Force.

ELEVEN

OWEN WAS STUNNED. Finding out she had taken flying lessons in high school had been a surprise, but not shocking. If that was what part of her school curriculum included, it wasn't exactly earth-shattering news.

But to discover his elderly grandmother really had been part of the Russian Air Force during World War II? It was almost beyond comprehension.

Nika reached over and touched his hand. *That* got his attention. Her hands were soft. Everything about her was lovely. Another question entered his head that had nothing to do with World War II. Was it possible for a seventeen-year-old boy to fall in love with a girl he'd only met a few hours ago?

It surely felt like it was possible to him.

"Hello, Owen, are you still on the train with me?" Nika waved a hand in front of his face.

"Sorry, just hard to picture Grandmother, only a few months older than me, enlisting as one of the first female combat pilots in the world."

"I know. And I'd like to talk about it, but we have to keep reading if we want to get all the way through her diary before we reach Moscow."

TWELVE

OUR TRAINING IS THRILLING, but it is also frustrating. Most of the male pilots and trainers do not want us here. I don't think it has so much to do with us being women. It is more that they are so short on planes. There are plenty of male pilots. I am not so sure those male pilots would be as willing as us girl pilots to use the old crop dusters and leftovers from World War I to go up against the German war machine, though. We are used to making do. Most of us are thrilled to be allowed to fight at all.

Our equipment is substandard, and they have no female flight gear to give us, so we are using male clothing. We do not complain publicly, but in private with each other at night, we do voice our annoyance at having to wear oversized men's clothing. Using our knowledge of thread, needle, buttons, and rolling up extra inches of cloth, we make it work. The worst is the male underwear. It is miserable. What we wouldn't give for proper female underwear!

Our training continues; one by one, some of us find out we will never be pilots. Either we do not have the right skills, or our vision is too poor, or many other weaknesses, both physical and mental. Even though we are flying old planes, there is not one plane to spare in all of Russia. The Germans already took out much of our Air Force in a surprise attack while our planes were still sitting on the ground.

I am grateful that I have not yet been eliminated as a pilot.

The second most important job is navigator. I pay attention to both jobs, so that if I can't be the pilot, I can at least fly in the backseat and help guide whoever is the pilot.

The Germans are gaining ground. More of my people escape to the east. I have not heard from my father and mother recently, and I worry if they are all right.

THIRTEEN

TODAY WAS A BIG DAY. It was announced that there would be three groups of us. The first group would be daytime fighters, the second group is daytime bombers, and the third group will be nighttime bombers.

It turns out that I have exceptional night vision. They have told me I will continue my training—but as a night bomber. I can't say this is good news. The planes given to us are the oldest out-of-date ones you can imagine. Mine will be a Polikarpov Po-2 biplane. The plane I am training on was built around 1935 that was used for crop dusting. This was not unexpected. We knew the best planes were being kept for the current trained male pilots.

I would enjoy having this plane for fun flying, but I can't imagine what good it would do against the might of the German Air Force. This plane is made of wood and fabric. The German planes are made of steel and fly so fast. We are putting our trust in our leaders to figure out the best strategy for us.

. . .

"So," Owen said, "you are telling me that my grandmother was looking at going up against the Germans in nothing more than a wood and cloth airplane? Either she is the bravest women I've ever known or just plain nuts!"

"You and I have never had live with our backs to the wall like they did," Nika said. "Who knows? Back then, you may have been willing to fight the Germans with rocks and sticks to protect your country and fellow citizens."

"I'd like to think I was that brave, but it's insanity to think that old crop dusting planes would do any good against those Germans fighters."

"True, but something must have gone right, or your lovely grandmother would not still be with us."

FOURTEEN

TODAY IS a day of sorrow for me. I have already had friends die from this awful war, but today was the worst so far, and yet I am afraid even worse is still to come. One of our new pilot trainees and a navigator were coming in for a landing. It was their first time to solo together.

Something went wrong on approach. We don't know if the pilot panicked, if something broke in the plane, or what, but something happened to cause the plane to flip over when they were about 500 feet from the ground, and they crashed. Emergency teams and everyone else around rushed to the field where they had crashed.

The fire was too big for us to get near enough to help them. I pray they died on impact and not in that fire. That is our worst fear, burning to death in our planes. We wanted to all go back to our barracks and mourn the death of our comrades, but our trainers would not let us.

"This could happen every day, and every hour in battle," they said.

"There is no time to mourn. You must train harder than ever for this not to happen to you."

At the time I thought they were being heartless, but as the day went on, I saw the wisdom in their process. There are no breaks; there is no time to mourn the dead. We will have plenty of time to cry for them after the war is over.

Nika looked up from the diary. "Can you imagine watching a friend die and having to keep going on and work as if nothing happened?"

"Not in today's world, but as you said, when their backs were against the wall, they had to adapt and do things they normally could not do. Grandmother's back was against the wall."

"How could your grandmother ever be so normal again after something like that?"

"I don't know," Owen said. "All I know is that I have never seen my grandmother be mean or spiteful. On the other hand, when my father was hurt in that wreck, she didn't break down. My mother is strong, but my grandmother is stronger. Even then, she just did what needed to be done."

"It is quite an honor to get to know her. I am glad you chose to wear tennis shoes on your trip," Nika said, "or I might not have stopped to chat with you."

"I'm glad, too," Owen said.

FIFTEEN

TONIGHT WAS OUR NIGHT. Our first night to fly a mission. Bragging that all my training had prepared me for this night would be a lie. Yes, technically I knew I was ready, but emotionally I was not.

It is one thing to say you are willing to die for your country, but the second you hear the gunfire and explosions from the antiaircraft fire, a knot in your stomach forms. I've heard these sounds from way off in the distance, but now I know I will be within inches of these bullets, shells, and explosions.

It was the longest sunset to wait for in my life, once I knew I would be flying my first mission that night. Late into the afternoon my navigator and I kept checking the sun's position. Although the wait was long, it is amazing to see how fast the sun moves when it is in relation to the ground. Once that sun kisses the ground, it flies so fast into darkness.

My navigator and I double-checked our plane. I made sure she was strapped in. We had been trained that this was necessary. We had a mission not long ago where a navigator's seat belt was not fastened correctly during training, and she almost fell out, so a rule was made that each pilot's routine included double-checking the navigator's seatbelt. A mechanic would check mine after I strapped in. Tonight those straps felt tight but reassuring.

My trusty Po-2 engine crackled to life. Everything was perfect for takeoff. We were one of forty planes flying that night. My navigator yelled through the tube that all was clear on her end. With a push of the throttle, we rushed down the short airstrip and were soon airborne.

Our mission tonight was to take out a supply train that was due to take supplies to the Germans. Our intelligence along the railroad had given us good information, and the train should be arriving anytime.

It only took fifteen minutes to fly to the German lines. In this first wave, there would be six of us. Three of the crews had flown the night before and already were acting like old veterans, as they tried to reassure us earlier before we took off.

The first two planes were a few minutes ahead of us. We could tell when they attacked—not by the sound of their explosion but by the hornet's nest that had been awakened.

The antiaircraft fire began, and it was heavy. The Germans did not know what was going on, since this was just the second day of our campaign of silent night bombing. They were shooting everywhere and in any direction.

We were with the second wave going in. Dodging the AA fire was a joke. All we could do was change altitude from time to time. The smoke and fumes from the AA fire was suffocating, but forward we went.

Finally, I saw the tracks and started following them. It was only a short distance before I saw the train. It apparently had stopped when the night fighting began. Unfortunately for them, we knew exactly where they were now.

I had decided to take out the engine if possible. I wanted to make sure that the engine could not go back to get more supplies or push the train back down the track, out of our reach of the limited fuel supply available on our plane.

I cut my engine to idle, and an eerie quietness took over, but it was short-lived. It was just the Germans reloading and looking up into the night sky for us. Once again it seemed there was a wall of bullets and exploding shells between us and that train, but my trusty Po-2 kept flying.

I could hear the "zing" of bullets. It felt like we had poked the hornets' nest, and poke that hornets' nest we continued to do. My training took over, and I lined up my bombing run on that train engine. I pulled the pin to release the bombs.

I didn't have time to watch if I had hit my target or not. I had to re-engage my engine and gain altitude again before I crashed. I heard the explosion behind me and hoped my aim was true. A few seconds later, my navigator yelled through the hose at me, "You hit it!"

I smiled. One hit for Mother Russia. I had done my job.

SIXTEEN

AFTER OUR FIRST night's mission, my navigator and I pretty much collapsed into our bunks. The adrenaline had drained out of our bodies. The impact of what we had done and what we had just lived through was starting to hit us.

As the sun rose, my navigator looked at me and suddenly started laughing.

"You should see your face," she said.

I looked at hers in the morning light and laughed as well. "Probably looks as bad as yours."

Our faces were dirty from oil from our engine and smoke from the exploding AA shells we had flown through. If we had not had glasses on, our eyes surely would have been damaged.

"I can't believe we made it through all those bullets and shells without getting hit," I said.

My navigator sobered. "I cannot believe we are still alive, either."

Unable to sleep, we decided to look over our plane in the daylight. I knew it had been bad, but I was shocked. When I saw the bullet holes and gashes from exploding shells, I nearly threw up. How had we managed to survive?

Our plane was full of little holes. How none of those pieces of small, deadly metal didn't hit either of us, I'll never know. My navigator and I didn't want to cry in front of the maintenance crew working over our plane, but we felt like it. The wonderment and relief were overwhelming.

There was a makeshift sink nearby where we washed off the oil and smoke from our faces. As I wiped it away, it felt as though all the innocence of my childhood was being wiped away as well.

It has only been one night, and I am already a battle-hardened combat pilot. I thought I would feel pride today; instead, I feel like I have the weight of an entire country on my shoulders. No eighteen-year-old should feel that. I pray no child of mine ever experiences such a heavy burden.

SEVENTEEN

Owen looked at Nika and she at him. Both slowly shook their heads in disbelief at what they had just read.

"I know I should feel pride in my grandmother, but all I can feel is sadness."

"Me as well."

"That image of her washing her face and losing her childhood will stay with me forever."

"When I wipe off my makeup at night, I sometimes feel like I'm wiping away the grown-up I pretend to be. Wiping away a night of battle and knowing you will do it night after night until the war ends or you die—what a terrible thing!"

They both stared out the window as the countryside passed by, lost in their own thoughts.

"I think I would like to wait a bit before we read any more," Owen broke the silence. "Right now, I just want to go see her and maybe give her a happy memory. Sometimes we play cards. Maybe she would like to play a little rummy."

"I have cards in my carry-on bag. I'll go get them."

While Nika went for her playing cards, Owen got another hot cup of tea and took it to Grandmother. She was awake, her seat was up, and she was looking out the window. She saw him and smiled. He handed her the tea.

"Thank you, Owen," she said. "You are a good grandson."

"I—I don't know what to say, Grandmother. Nika is doing a good job of translating your diary. Discovering what you went through is hard for me to hear. I can hardly bear to think of you going through all that."

"But I survived," Grandmother said. "And here I am today enjoying my train ride and eating cake with my favorite grandson."

"I'm your only grandson," Owen reminded her.

"That does not mean you cannot be my favorite," she teased.

Nika arrived with her cards. It took some coordination to set up the game, but grandmother was happy to play a few hands. It had been quite a while since they had played, and he had been much younger. She was better than he remembered. Apparently, she was easy on him back home. Both Owen and Nika got soundly beat.

As she piled up the points, he joked that he was going to leave her at the next train station if she didn't let him win once. She retorted that she would still beat him to Moscow.

"I didn't know my grandma could trash talk," he said, in a loud whisper to Nika.

"Not knowing about your grandmother and her talents is turning into a theme on this trip, I think," Nika whispered back.

Grandmother could hear every word and grinned as she gathered up the cards and expertly shuffled.

"Hey! I'm making up for it now…by letting her win."

"Really?" Grandmother said. "Letting me win? I don't think so, rookie."

After they'd counted the points from the last hand, it was clear that Nika had lost even worse than Owen.

"I guess the loser should buy the winners' dinner," Nika said. "What can I get for you two?"

"Not dinner," Grandmother said. "I wouldn't mind another cup of tea, though."

"You drink any more tea, you'll need to go to the *tualet* again," Owen said.

Grandmother sighed dramatically. "I hope that isn't the *only* Russian word you learn on this trip."

As Nika went to get some tea and snacks for them all, Grandmother and Owen had a chance to talk.

"I like that girl," she said. "Reminds me of me when I was young."

"I'm definitely not bored anymore," Owen said. "She has made this trip a lot of fun."

"Make sure you get her, what is the word, digits, yes, digits—that's the word I'm looking for."

"You mean her phone number?" Owen said. "Where in the world did you learn the term *digits?*"

"I still teach, remember? The young men at the college are always talking about getting a girl's digits. I thought they were being disrespectful until they explained."

"It's still a bit embarrassing to have my grandmother trying to set me up!"

Grandmother laughed. "Life is short; never put off till tomorrow what you need to do today. The war taught me that lesson."

Nika returned with tea and sandwiches. Grandmother said something in Russian to her. Nika laughed, but her face grew red.

"What did my grandmother say to you?"

"She said that you want my digits but are too shy to ask, so I needed to make sure I give them to you before I leave the train."

Owen felt his own face growing red. Having his grandmother play matchmaker on this trip was not something he had anticipated. Nothing about this trip was anything he had anticipated.

EIGHTEEN

WORD CAME in that they were looking for volunteers to fly a day mission. It turned out we had Russian troops surrounded by the Germans. Our men were low on everything. They needed food, water, and most importantly ammo.

Since our small planes could land almost anywhere, those in charge thought we might have the best chance of getting it to them. Dropping supplies by parachute was too risky, because if we missed the target even a little, it might mean that the ammunition would go to the Germans, and we knew their supplies were low as well.

Since this would be a day mission, navigators would not be needed. The pilot would be able to navigate by sight. Not carrying the navigator would lighten the plane enough that we could add precious more weight to the supplies we could carry. Each day, we were to leave at first light, and if we could, we would fly back and forth and back and forth. No guns, no bombs, no parachute—nothing except supplies strapped to our planes. I even considered not eating anything so that a few more bullets could be loaded, but the chance of passing out from exhaustion was too great. I could not risk starving myself.

Our first day began. The biggest threat we faced was the German pilots. At night, all we had to worry about was the searchlights finding us and the German fighters shooting us down before we could get to the antiaircraft guns. In daylight, their fighter pilots could see for miles. We chose to fly as close to the ground as possible.

I was selected to fly third. We took off every few minutes. I knew where we were going. My instructions were: Follow the river, look for a town, fly ten kilometers west of that town, and I should see our flag flying.

I kept an eye out for fighters, as well as smoke from anyone ahead of me who might have been shot down. My plane ran smoothly—always a good thing since my life depended on it. Finally, I saw the town. I was told to stay away from it since the Germans had most likely overran it by today.

I cut west. As close to the ground as I was, I could hear occasional guns and explosions going off, so I knew I was going the correct direction. Finally, I saw approximately where I was supposed to land. I saw the Russian flag ripped to shreds, but it was still flying high enough for me to see.

The field I was supposed to land in was so small. A couple of Russian soldiers ran out of the woods and waved at me. I circled around as tight as I could, checking out the landing field, hoping there would be no surprise holes in the runway to rip my landing gear from my plane.

It was tight, but my landing was perfect. The field was smooth except where artillery shells had landed on the edges of the trees.

About eight men came running up to my plane after I came to a stop. One of them shouted, "Comrade, we are so glad to see you!" I climbed out of my seat and took off my helmet.

The shock of seeing a woman left them speechless for a moment.

"Do you want to stand there staring at me, or do you want the supplies?" I said. "More planes are right behind me, so we have to unload fast!"

They blinked and closed their mouths.

"Sorry." One of the soldiers gallantly took my hand and kissed it. "We weren't expecting a beautiful angel to drop from heaven and deliver supplies."

Under normal conditions, I would have blushed, but neither of us had the luxury of time for me to do so.

I heard the familiar sound of another Po-2 coming in.

"Another angel coming in," I said. "We have to hurry!"

By the time we unloaded my plane, the second one had landed. I saw it was Alexandra.

"What happened?" I yelled. "I thought you would be here by now."

"German fighter spotted us," Alexandra yelled back. "Took us a while to shake him. He finally gave up, but be careful, there are sharks in the water up there, and they are ready to strike."

I started my plane, gave Alexandra a salute, and took off. Luckily, I did not get spotted by any German fighter. I noticed that Alexandra's plane had some bullet holes in it. Alexandra was beautiful. A natural blonde with pale skin. She definitely looked like an angel—one with bullet holes in her wings.

We each made about five runs that day. We found out later those troops were able to break free of being surrounded and retook the town that had fallen to the Germans. Knowing I had a part in that made me feel so proud.

"I can just imagine the look on those guys' faces seeing some young girl flying in," Owen said.

"Just imagine flying across enemy lines in the daylight, landing in a small field, and delivering those supplies to those men. I mean, the men were brave for not giving up and keeping on fighting, but knowing they were all alone and this little speck comes flying out of the sky and some girl delivers what they need to keep fighting…"

"I know. Humbling to think about it. I get upset because sometimes I can't recharge my cell phone immediately."

"Me, too. It definitely puts things in perspective."

NINETEEN

Tonight my plane was down for repairs, and the parts are supposed to arrive tomorrow. I hate not flying tonight, but I can still do my part by helping the ground crew. This gave me a real chance to see our fight from another point of view.

It gave me a whole new respect for the ground crews and what they do. It let me understand better why we are able to fly about forty planes a night —even more missions than our male counterparts.

On average, each flight crew flies eight missions a night. Of course, we all try to fly more than that, but bullet holes in our fabric, as well as our engines, pilots, and navigators can ground a plane for a while.

My personal best is fifteen missions in one night. I hope to beat that! Tonight is my personal worst at zero missions.

Watching the ground crew is almost like watching the Ballet in Moscow. A plane will come in. Even before it comes to a stop, I hear some of the other pilots beating the sides of the plane, screaming "More bombs, more bombs!" Usually someone will rush the pilot and navigator something to drink or a bite to eat. It's always about how to squeeze in one more mission before daylight.

As the seasons change and the nights are shorter, we can only maybe fit in four or five missions. On the longer nights, we can do eight to twelve or even more, depending on how close we are to the targets.

I can see better how our "friendly" competition with men's units means we are beating their numbers. Official Russian doctrine means teams only work on specific planes. So, a lot of time is wasted on teams waiting to find out which plane has landed, and the reloading team services that plane.

Our philosophy is that it does not matter what plane comes in. If you are refueling, you refuel whatever plane comes in. If you are an armorer, you will be putting bombs on whatever plane comes in.

We are turning planes around in four to five minutes. It is very much like how a tank assembly line runs. Everyone has a job, and it's almost like the plane never stops moving when it comes in, much like a tank on a conveyor belt. Plane is refueled, rearmed, oil added, checked for damage, slapped on the tail, and off it goes!

Much to the amusement and frustration to the men's units nearby, we are surpassing them every night now in number of missions.

TWENTY

THE PAST TWO *weeks have been quite a thrill for us ladies. We have been sharing an airstrip with a unit of men fighter pilots. We both know we have jobs to do, but the chance to actually talk or even flirt a little with a man was something we all had missed.*

For the first day or so, we were like a show for the men to watch in the evenings, like a trained animal act at the circus. But when they saw us keep going up time and time again, they began to respect us.

They started coming over during the night, helping us with whatever they could. It actually was nice having them help with lifting some of the bombs. They are so heavy. It was one of these nights my plane was down again for repairs, so I was able to interact with them.

One young man caught my eye. He was about four inches taller than me. Hair as black as night, a cute dimple on his chin, and a smile that could charm anyone. He needed a haircut, but it was his dark, brown eyes that captured my attention. I saw the respect in them, and the kindness.

My heart fluttered when he introduced himself as "Andrius." He didn't talk much, but he seem to always be there all night long working near or beside me. We made a little small talk, but nothing deep. I was smitten but figured he couldn't be all that interested in a girl dressed in a badly fitting uniform with her faced smudged with oil and smoke.

Still, during the next few days, he always seemed to be standing near my plane when I came in to rearm for the next mission. One evening we were eating our breakfast, which would have been dinnertime for the men, and Andrius came over and sat by me. I have no idea what I ate or even if I ate anything at that meal, but we finally had a real conversation. He was shy but very intelligent, sweet, and caring.

We discussed what we wanted to do after the war. I let him know I wanted to study to be an aeronautical engineer or a test pilot. He grinned big, for it was his dream to become an aeronautical engineer as well.

We both knew that our units would be moving onto different airfields soon, and we exchanged addresses to look up each other in Moscow after the war. However, I hinted I wouldn't mind him visiting before he left. We girls were absolutely forbidden from going to the male side of the airfield.

That night went on without a hitch. However, the next day I didn't see him. Nor did I see him that night. Another day passed, and again I did not see him. Had I scared him off, or was he simply transferred to a different location?

Finally, I asked one of the other men who had been hanging around. He seemed upset by the question. "I wished you had not asked about Andrius; he was our finest pilot and instructor."

It occurred to me that I had never realized what his job was. Now I found out that he was the finest pilot of his unit, as well as an instructor.

"I watched the whole thing from my plane," his friend continued. "We had a bomber come under attack by four German fighters, and it was damaged badly. Andrius dove into the middle of the German fighters and attacked in order to give the bomber and its crew a fighting chance to either get away or bail out. It was one of the bravest things I've ever seen."

I almost wished Andrius' friend would stop talking. It hurt to hear these things, but the man had more to say.

"The Germans were on him like hornets. Andrius made his plane do things our instructors said our planes could not do. He immediately shot one of the planes out of the sky. It exploded into a huge fireball. All the while, the other three shot into him. He went after the second one. I saw smoke pour out of it as it raced away from the fight, but by then the other two fighters were too much.

"I saw his plane on fire. He was going down fast. We never saw a parachute. The last bomber in our formation saw an explosion from a distance. He said it was Andrius' plane hitting the ground."

"Oh no!" I could hardly believe the young man I had begun a friendship with was already gone. "What happened then?"

"We sent crews to the crash site as soon as we could. Nothing was left; the impact was so hard, the fire so intense, it incinerated everything. All that was left were bits of metal from his wings. His family will be awarded a medal, but they have no body to bury. His personal belongings were sent home yesterday. I'm sorry I'm the one to tell you this."

I couldn't help it. I went back to my cot and wept. I sobbed until I was sick and throwing up. I didn't realize how much that sweet young man had grown in my heart in those few weeks I had worked with him. I think learning of his death was also the final straw that broke open the shell I'd formed around my heart for the girls we had lost, for whom I had not allowed myself to grieve. I cried so hard for so long that our flight medic came to check on me to make certain I was flight-worthy. I assured her I was.

Ten thousand Roman gladiators could not keep me from flying that night.

I made sure to wash up and focused hard during the briefing. We looked at our targets on the map. I specifically asked for the ammo supply or the headquarters. No one dared challenge me on targets this night.

My navigator had to be the bravest woman on earth to be willing to fly with me. I think everyone thought I had a death wish. Far from it. I wanted the Germans to know who I was and who they were dealing with this night.

They wanted to call me a Night Witch? I would be the witch of their nightmares this night.

Our bombing runs started. The Germans were ready, so we had to soften their defenses first. The planes in front of me took out as many searchlights and antiaircraft fire as they could, but still too many survived, and I had to waste my first run in taking out a searchlight.

For all my anger, my navigator was an angel in my ear. She talked to me through the communication hose, reminding me we would get to my targets tonight but to be patient. I wanted to scream, but my training was strong, and I listened.

Bombing run two, same thing, had to work on the lights and antiaircraft guns. Bombing run three, same thing.

Finally, bombing run four, I burst through their lines like a lion chasing its prey. There still was some antiaircraft fire going on, but I stayed focused. I could see where the ammo supply target was. I swooped in and unloaded my bombs. To my disappointment, my bombs fell short. I started my engine back up. Back to base we went.

Bombing run five, I was able to hit the target, but there was no big explosion. Again, with bombing run six, I hit the target but no critical damage. The only thing keeping me from doing a suicide mission was knowing I had another human life in my plane.

I so wanted revenge for Andrius and all the other friends we had lost. They were all so young, like me. Andrius just wanted to fly and build airplanes. He didn't ask for this war. He didn't ask the Germans to come marching toward his home in Moscow.

I do not believe in superstition. Never have and never will, but on bombing run seven, I had a moment of doubt. Lucky bomb run seven. Again, we went in. Crossed the front lines and cut our engine to idle. All was silent. I could see my target once again.

My angel, my navigator kept talking to me. Stay calm, Klara. Remember to breathe. Stay steady. We will hit something that will start a chain reaction with this run.

Maybe the adrenaline was finally running out of me, maybe the rage, who knows? But finally, I was back in my zone. Able to shut out the sounds of ground fire, the sounds of the antiaircraft fire.

I was gliding in. Waiting, waiting, waiting, and finally released the bombs over what looked like a sweet spot. I kicked in my engine and roared up as fast as I could. Thank goodness I did. The explosion that followed about blew us out of the sky. I had finally hit the sweet spot. The explosion was so great, I had to keep all my focus on keeping my plane in the sky.

My navigator was yelling what she could see. The size of the fireball and then the small secondary explosions happening. She kept saying, "So much less ammo that can be used against our boys! We did it, Klara, we did it!"

I was not satisfied; I wanted to lay a few bombs down the throat of the commander of this location. The man who had sent four fighters to pounce on my Andrius. I flew back to my base as fast as I could. I was now one of those pilots banging on my side, "More bombs! More bombs!"

The morning was coming. There wasn't much night left for bombing runs, and I knew it. Off we went again. I did let the navigator fly a little toward the front lines, so I could close my eyes a bit and rest. I don't know if I actually rested, but it seemed a very short time before she was yelling at me that it was time for me to take over.

Back into the lions' den we went. However, its roar was much less this time. I could still see the orange glow of the ammo supply burning.

I loved it.

I now turned my focus on the HQ. I don't think they were expecting another aggressive run after us hitting the ammo dump. I risked it all on this run. If our intelligence was correct, I knew about where the entrance was. It would be a one in 10,000 shot, but it was worth it to try.

My navigator did not know my plan. I knew by now I only had time for one more run before daylight. I circled around. The Germans knew I was up in the dark somewhere; they just did not know where.

I cut the engine and dove. I dove harder and faster than I ever had before. It seemed every machine gun the Germans possessed was pointed to the sky, firing randomly looking for me, even though other planes were around. Some came close and sounded like bees flying by. Some did not just fly by, and I heard them smack into my plane's canvas.

The point past safety, I pulled on my stick and released the bombs, right at the entrance of the HQ. I could actually see the faces of some of the Germans as I flew by. They were lit by fires from previous bombing runs.

Once again, I kicked in the engine and flew up. My bombs landed true, I knew that, but I did not know how well. I would not find out until later if my bombs hit or missed their mark.

I flew back to base. My navigator was silent. I knew she was mad at me. I took a very dangerous unnecessary risk. I endangered our plane and our lives, primarily for revenge.

Yes, we were ready to die for our country, but there was a difference between being willing to die and suicide. I had come within inches of committing suicide and taking my navigator with me. I landed at our base and slowly climbed out of my plane. A ground crew ran up to help us. I fell to my knees exhausted.

It was then I realized the ground crew was helping my navigator out of her seat. She had been wounded and was losing blood. It was my fault. I had flown too low. I stood up to help.

Even though she was weak, she had enough strength to slap me. What hurt the most is that I deserved it.

"This war is bigger than you, Klara!" she said. "Bigger than Andrius. Russia needs you, this plane, and believe it or not, Russia even needs me. Get over yourself and your dead boyfriend, and be a soldier."

With those words she collapsed. They rushed her to medical.

At that moment the blood lust of anger lifted from my eyes. I realized blind rage and revenge is not me. It is not who I am.

I am tough. I am a fighter. I will protect the weak, but I will never again blindly endanger the ones I love.

I found out later that my glorious bombing runs were less than glorious. Yes, I had made a huge fire ball, but it turns out I had hit fuel. Yes, it did hurt them a little, but it was not the huge impact I had hoped for. And the bombing run that ended my navigator's flying career? I missed the HQ completely and hit the Germans' latrine.

TWENTY-ONE

IT HAD TO HAPPEN SOMETIME. I had beat the odds for far too long. My plane had taken a beating, but I had not actually been wounded until tonight. A German fighter intercepted us. We were caught in a searchlight that had been hidden and then turned on after we had crossed enemy lines.

At the last moment, my navigator saw the fire coming from the machine gun of the plane and screamed at me to take evasive maneuvers. I cut my speed and did a tight turn.

The German planes cannot fly as slowly as ours or turn as fast. As I slammed the plane hard to the left, something hit the side of the plane. It hurt my arm and leg badly. But I didn't have time to think about the pain. I was too busy trying to save our lives.

I made my Po-2 spin like it never had before. The German pilot flew past me very fast. I don't know how we missed each other in the air. He tried to slow and spin in the same pattern with me. He knew our plane was wounded from his machine gun fire.

I must have had more flying hours than him, because he did not pay attention to his plane speed, and his engine shut off. His plane dove to the ground, and I lost sight of it in the darkness, but I did see the "poof" of his parachute in the distance as it blotted out stars and he was momentarily caught in the flash of a searchlight.

By now my arm and leg were absolutely burning. I reached over and felt with my right hand. I felt wetness. I knew it had to be blood. I went ahead and dropped my bombs on what appeared to be a minor target so we could fly back to base faster and use less fuel.

I told my navigator that I was wounded and to be ready to take over the controls if I passed out. I didn't know how bad I was hit. There was a chance I wouldn't even make it back to base, but I was able to stay awake the whole way and landed well enough not to damage my plane.

My navigator screamed for a medic, and one came running over as they helped me out. As luck would have it, I had been shot twice. Fortunately, they were not much more than scratches compared to what some of the girls had endured. They were deep but could heal without permanent damage. I was grounded for a few days but was able to fly again shortly thereafter.

"I've seen those two scars on her left arm," Owen said. "I figured it was from ironing or cooking!"

"Oh, so your sweet old grandma could only have domestic housewife scars?" Nika said.

"Seriously, who would guess that she had sustained bullet wounds?"

"I know!" Nika said. "I would have thought the same thing."

TWENTY-TWO

WE HAVE BEEN FLYING missions all night long. Things were pretty routine. It was just the regular amount of ground fire and antiaircraft fire.

We got a report from one of our teams coming in. They informed us that suddenly three of our planes just burst into flames and fell from the sky. They couldn't understand what happened.

Finally, it dawned on them that it was the special trained German night fighters coming after them. The team that made it back was the fourth plane flying in that night, with a fifth behind them.

They dove to the ground as close as they could, and they heard the bullets firing at the planes, but they were just out of reach. However, the fifth plane—the one that was behind them—didn't realize what was going on. The German fighter went in after easier prey. The navigator looked back and saw that the fifth plane had also gone down. Four planes downed in one night. Only one had made it back.

Our commander canceled the missions for the rest of the night to get a strategy together. It seemed an impossibility. We were good pilots, but our planes were no match against these German night fighters.

Arrangements were made tonight for Russian night fighters to help give us some defense, but we lost eight good women last night. Eight of our friends, eight daughters, eight sisters, wives, mothers, all gone. It will take us quite a while to recover from last night. Morale is low, but we intend to keep going on. We'll keep flying our missions. We'll keep giving it back to the Germans night after night. We will be relentless. It gives us great pleasure to know that we are, at the very least, giving these Germans nightmares—never knowing when one of us might swoop in and drop a bomb on their head.

The only weakness in our strategy is that because of the size of the planes, our bombs are not all that large. Going after the really hard targets is kind of pointless, because the bombs our planes are able to carry cannot penetrate reinforced targets. We are, however, an excellent harassment campaign, and we frequently do hit the soft targets.

Another thing we do is make them lose sleep. The fact that they never know when we will silently swoop in keeps them from ever getting a peaceful night's rest. I envision right before they drift off to sleep, one of our bombs goes off, and suddenly they are forced awake to run to the bunkers, take cover, and man their weapons.

Every minute of sleep they do not get means that during the day they are less effective, less able to focus, less able to aim true and concentrate. Hopefully, it gives our Russian soldiers an edge.

We go after the soft targets of vehicles. Supply trucks, motorcycles, searchlights, ammo storage places that are not fortified, houses they might be hiding in, anything we can do to inflict damage, injuries, and death. Anything we can do to soften them up for our Russian men, brothers, sons, and fathers, who have poorer equipment and less of it than the Germans.

For every bomb we drop, it means just one more little advantage we can give our brothers-in-arms. Our bombs may be small, our damage might be small, but our overall impact is large, when German soldiers must go hungry or thirsty because we blew up their supplies. If they also have to ration their bullets because we destroyed those as well, then our little bombs are a great success.

Nika stopped translating for a few minutes. "I need to stop awhile and just absorb what I'm reading. This diary is—how do you say?—mind-blowing."

"I know," Owen said. "Those women flew into great danger even when the least they could do was disrupt the German soldier's sleep. I can see that it could make a difference, though. I know how miserable I feel in the morning when my dog wakes me up several times in the middle of the night barking at some cat he sees through the window."

"I confess I am not the most pleasant of personalities if I have gone a long time without sleep," Nika admitted.

"I can't imagine you grumpy in the morning."

"Trust me. Grumpy me with bedhead is a sight to behold."

Owen thought she would be beautiful no matter what.

"The Germans must have been exhausted," Owen said. "All night long, unable to hear the planes coming, bombs going off, constantly moving forward or backwards, unable to build a permanent base, to build anywhere truly safe from the bombs, then dealing with the regular Russian land army attacking day or night, and they were so far from home."

"Yes," Nika said. "Not all the Germans were bad. A lot of them were just boys drafted into military service. Sons, brothers, and fathers who wanted to go home themselves. But many of the German soldiers were cruel to the Russian people, and that is why the people fought so hard against them."

Owen ran his hand over the ragged cover of the diary. "Well, obviously the Russians won, or we would not be sitting here on the train together."

"It took many countries working together to stop the Germans, but it was my Mother Russia that suffered the heaviest losses."

TWENTY-THREE

Today was a different mission for me. Last night we lost a plane; however, the pilot flying near them said they never saw a crash. We hoped that they had been able to land because their plane was damaged by enemy fire or mechanical failure.

Another pilot and I flew during the day to the approximate spot where they were last seen. We hoped they would signal us or at least we could somehow find out if they had crashed or not.

We flew without our navigators, so that if we found them alive we could fly them back out again. It is amazing to fly in the day, especially when no one is shooting at you. So many details you don't see at night. The other pilot and I signaled each other when we had reached the approximate spot. Then we started flying in a grid pattern.

How thankful I was when we saw their plane in a field. They were waving at us. Luckily, we were able to land. It turned out it was a mechanical problem, and they made an emergency landing.

We were able to load them up and take them back, and then we flew two mechanics in to fix the plane and get it back to base. Our friends were fine, although shaken up. They had been afraid the Nazis would discover them, but fortunately they were far enough behind enemy lines that they had not been found.

TWENTY-FOUR

THE TRAIN CONTINUED to rumble along the route. Klara was grateful that Owen had found a young friend to spend time with. It gave her the freedom to be alone with her thoughts. She needed time to sort out her emotions and her memories.

So much time had passed since she had last seen her home country. It was strange to think of herself as she had been when she was a young woman but see a gray-haired woman staring back at her in the reflection of the window.

Klara loved the fact that even though Owen was enjoying spending time with Nika, he still frequently came to check on her. The boy was growing into a fine and thoughtful man. She knew this because of something she'd seen a few months ago that she had never told him about. It was such a little thing, but it spoke to what kind of man he was and would be.

She had gone with his mother to a doctor's appointment. It

had been a lovely day. While Klara waited on her daughter-in-law, she decided to take a long walk around the park that was across from the medical office. There was a bench she could sit at and watch the people and traffic.

At a particularly busy intersection, there was a disheveled man with a sign "Homeless. Anything Helps." She watched a group of teenagers drive by and throw a drink at him. He shrugged it off like it was something that happened every day. But it was what happened next that made Klara sit up and pay attention.

A few cars behind those teenagers, another one stopped and put its hazard lights on. She recognized the car. It was a bright yellow Volkswagen bug. She had seen it a couple hours earlier when one of Owen's friends stopped by the house and picked him up for basketball practice.

Owen jumped out of the car, ran a few feet to the homeless man, and handed him what looked like a bag of fast food that Owen had probably just bought himself. He also handed the man one of his fresh towels he always had with him when he was playing ball.

Owen patted the man on the back and shook his head as if to say, "Sorry about my idiot generation, here is what little food I have, and here is a towel to wipe off that liquid." And with a flash, Owen was back in his friend's car and driving off to keep from blocking traffic any longer than they had to.

Klara saw the homeless man watch the yellow Volkswagen until it was out of sight. Then he finally looked away, shook his head in disbelief, and smiled with bliss as he closed his eyes and took a bite of the sandwich that had been in the bag.

It was a selfish memory that Klara kept to herself. She did not want Owen to ever think she was spying on him.

Although a stranger, Nika was also impressing her. During the war, Klara had learned to size up people quickly. The intervening years had only polished that ability. Within minutes she could usually tell if they were good, bad, or allowing themselves to just occupy space on Planet Earth for a short time and for no particular reason.

Klara saw the outer beauty of Nika. The girl was quite lovely, but more importantly, Klara saw what was on the inside— another young person with a kind heart. She had a feeling that Nika was also the rare kind of person who would stop traffic to help a homeless person.

Klara thought that maybe she should keep nudging this budding relationship a little as they continued on their journey. Who knew? She was not much older than Owen when she fell in love.

TWENTY-FIVE

I AM SO grateful I am able to write in the diary again. I thought my last entry had already been written. Three days ago, on a bombing run, I was shot down.

"Whoa," Owen interrupted Nika. "My grandmother was shot down?"

"That is what it says. Now if you would stop interrupting me, I can get to the details."

An antiaircraft shell went off near my plane. Shrapnel hit my engine and took it out. We went down, and there was nothing I could do. Luckily there was a small road where I was able to crash-land. Our plane flipped on its nose, and there it stuck.

I was knocked out a few minutes. My navigator woke me up as she was climbing down to the ground. I was alive, but what a headache I had! She helped me out. Already a knot was forming on my forehead.

We knew we had to run. We were too close to enemy lines.

The only weapon I carried was my sidearm. We headed east. We saw no one, but we did see German fighters flying in the sky. When we would see or hear them, we would hide.

Word had gotten to us that any Nazi who killed a Night Witch would be awarded the Iron Cross. Yes, we were proud of the fact that we were so hated by them, but it was still frightening to think what they would do to us if we were captured.

One of the few funny things we have heard in this awful war is that the German soldiers are convinced that we have supernatural powers. They believe we receive special injections that give us catlike night vision. We love to laugh at this one, although it would be nice if it were true.

We drank water out of the streams we crossed. For two nights, we endured the cold and huddled together to keep warm.

On the third day, we were walking and then heard voices. We drew our guns, ready to shoot if necessary. Then I realized we were hearing Russian being spoken. Several Russian soldiers poked their heads up from a ditch they were positioned in. I had never been so grateful to see a fellow countryman. They were so well hidden that we had almost walked on top of them.

By now the Russian men knew who the Night Witches were, and we had their gratitude! They quickly got us to some warmth and food. It was amazing to be treated with such respect, after having to beg to be allowed to join the military. In spite of being exhausted, cold, and hungry, we were privately proud to have earned that kind of admiration.

It turns out we were only about ten miles from our base, and these men were able to drive us there. Oh, the rejoicing that happened when we drove up. When our friends had found our plane, but no one was around, they feared the worst. They thought the Nazis must have gotten us. They had even started packing up our stuff to send home to our families. Thank goodness we got back before then. My mother would have died of a broken heart.

I am glad to be alive, but that was a good Po-2, and it was damaged beyond repair. I now have to get used to a different one.

"Stop reading for a minute," Owen said. "I need some time to absorb this. My eighteen-year-old grandmother was shot down, knocked out, eluded Nazis for days in unfamiliar territory, got back to base—and her only complaint was she couldn't fly her old plane?"

Nika nodded. "I am honored to have had the opportunity to meet this Night Witch grandmother of yours."

"Me, too," Owen said, thoughtfully. "Me, too."

TWENTY-SIX

"THERE ARE STILL a few more pages in the diary," Nika said. "Shall we finish them or go check on your grandmother?"

"I would like to finish the diary. Then I want to go check on my grandmother. I have many questions for her," Owen said.

"I'm glad you said that," Nika said. "I feel the same way."

And once again, she began to read.

Rumors of the war ending are entering our conversation during downtime while eating or waiting on bad weather to clear. Some of us are afraid to speak of the possibility, for fear that we might somehow accidentally upset the direction of the war.

The Americans and British are advancing from the east, and we seem to be moving west every day. I know it is a good day when we pack up our "base" to move further west away from Moscow.

The Germans are falling apart. They are not used to our geography and climate. When we drive or fly, we see tanks and trucks abandoned in deep mud. Some damaged. Some buried too deep to move. The worst is seeing the makeshift graves for both sides. Who knows if those men will ever receive a proper burial? I'm tired of seeing them.

The German soldiers we now see are nothing more than young boys. Hitler has to be at his end. Sending such young ones to fight. But surrender has not come, and bullets do not know age.

We continue to do our bombing runs at night. I hope that all we are doing is to make them run back to Germany faster. But there is nowhere safe for them now. Once the United States entered the war, it was only a matter of time. The German Air Force is down to almost nothing. I suspect most of their remaining planes have been pulled back to protect Berlin.

We do find pockets of Germans unwilling to give up. I wonder if their nearly defeated soldiers fear going back to face Hitler more than they fear us. Our bombing runs will continue until no German is left on Russian soil.

TWENTY-SEVEN

Today is like no other. Germany has surrendered. It was a day of great joy, but one of confusion for some of us. What do we do now? We have been bombing and flying every day for so long. How do we turn off that switch and go about doing normal things once again?

I suspect we will pack up and travel back to Moscow and go our separate ways soon. Maybe never to see each other again. For the first time, I had the opportunity to sleep at night instead of doing bombing runs. It felt strange. Still, I was able to doze a bit and enjoyed getting up early that next morning.

I took a walk to a small stream. It was barely dawn. I sat at that stream and put my toes in the water. It was in the early part of May, and the water had not yet warmed up. In fact, it was freezing, but it felt luxurious to do something as normal as taking off my heavy boots and dipping my toes in the water. It felt strange that I could finally do so without fear of being attacked. We had been on red alert for far too long. Although my mind told me that Germany had surrendered, my body had trouble believing it.

As I sat there, enjoying God's nature, the sun started to rise. It was a sun that was rising on a Russia that was free from German attack. No other day had felt like that.

I cried as the sun rose. I mourned all my friends who had been killed or wounded. I cried at the scars on my body from bullets that had come so close to killing me. I cried at the scars within my body of having to participate in the horror of war at such a young age. I cried for the young men my bombs had killed—many who had probably possessed no real desire to fight but had been forced to. But my sad tears eventually became tears of joy and hope. I had survived the war. I would be going home soon.

TWENTY-EIGHT

Owen, Nika, and Grandmother sat together at a table in the dining car, waiting for their dinner to be served.

"Thank you for letting us to read your diary, Grandmother," Owen said. "But why didn't you ever tell me any of this?"

Grandmother stayed silent a long time as she thought about her answer. Owen and Nika were respectful enough not to interrupt.

After a few moments, Klara spoke. "As bad as the things in the diary are, there are some details that I deliberately chose not to put in it."

"Why not?"

"Because I thought if I did not describe them, I would not remember them. I did not *want* to remember them. What I did not realize was that those details are the ones that I cannot forget. Believe me, I have tried."

"Like what kind of details?"

"Like what it feels like to see a friend running away from a plane she has managed to land that is in flames—and she is also in flames."

"I'm so sorry," Owen said. "I should not have asked."

"True," Grandmother said, "you should not have asked. Those kinds of memories are my burden to carry—not yours. God forbid that it should ever become yours."

"Does Dad know any of this?"

"No."

"Why not?"

"A mother's first instinct—and it is a good instinct—is to protect her child from all the evils in this world. I experienced a great evil. When your father was small, I would never have brought such horror into his life by telling him what I had endured during the war. Time passed. He grew into a fine man. The nightmares I dealt with after the war had pretty much ceased. I knew he would be curious and ask many questions. I was afraid that talking about it might bring the nightmares back. I preferred to pretend—even to myself—that it had never happened."

"But you are talking about it with us now," Owen said. "Why?"

"I have been torn about what to do. Although I never wanted to relive my part in the war, I also did not want to destroy the record of what my sister Night Witches and I had accomplished. My diary has not seen daylight for many years, but when the word of a reunion came to me, I pulled it out and read it again. It struck me anew how remarkable it all was, this story of what we young girls did for our country."

"I have certainly been inspired by it," Nika said.

"I'm glad, because there is still great evil in the world. I pray that neither of you will ever have to face something as terrible as we did, but if you do…I think it might be a good thing to know that it is possible for ordinary people to find extraordinary courage when it is necessary. Even young girls who would have rather been curling their hair and looking at fashion magazines somehow found the courage to fight back. One thing I learned and never forgot was that when one's back is against the wall, it is possible to fight harder and more effectively than you ever dreamed, no matter who you are."

They grew quiet as the waiter brought their dinner on thick china plates. After he left, Klara waited quietly with her hands in her lap. Owen knew what she was waiting for, and she knew that he knew. He had enjoyed many meals at her table. His grandmother was not only brave, she was a woman of faith. There was never a meal shared in her house without someone giving thanks to the God who had created it. He now believed that he understood a little better her insistence on this. It wasn't just for the food. It was also because of her gratitude that she was alive to enjoy it.

"Owen?" she asked, bowing her head and waiting for him to say grace.

"I would love to, Grandmother," he said. And he meant it.

TWENTY-NINE

"I wish I could have known Grandpa," Owen said, after they had finished dinner and returned to their seats.

"Yes," Grandmother said. "He died too soon. We should have had a few more years together. But those we had were good ones."

"How did you two meet?"

Grandmother got a faraway look in her eyes and, for some reason, decided to speak only in Russian. Owen thought perhaps it was because she had allowed herself to be transported back into time, or perhaps she was simply tired. Sometimes she did that if the day had been too long. She would start to speak in Russian and then catch herself and switch to English.

This time, however, Nika was there, and her eyes grew wide as she listened to whatever it was that Grandmother had said. Her hand reached for Owen's as though seeking reassurance or comfort.

Grandmother paused.

"Your grandmother says we already know how they met."

"How's that possible?" he asked.

"She says we know because we have read her diary."

"I can tell you are tired, Grandmother," he said. "Do you want for us to let you alone to rest, or do you want some tea, so that we can continue this conversation in English?"

"I lapsed into Russian again, didn't I?" she said. "Yes, I want to continue the conversation. Please bring me more of that good Russian tea if you don't mind."

"I don't mind at all."

After he returned, and she had sipped the hot tea for a bit, Grandmother seemed renewed and said, "Yes, I'm sure it was in there; Andrius was part of a fighter group that helped us for a few weeks."

Finally, it clicked for Owen.

"You mean the same Andrius who took on four German fighters was my grandfather? That Andrius? How is that possible?"

Grandmother's eyes twinkled, "Not even Germany's finest fighter pilots could take out my Andrius. I guess I didn't put that happy part in my diary since it was after the war and I had stopped writing in it."

Once again, she started speaking in Russian. Then she realized what she was doing and quickly switched back to English. She was weary from the trip, but her eyes were that of a woman in love, as she told them her love story.

"The war had ended. A year had passed, and we were all trying to rebuild our lives. I went back to Moscow to stay with my parents. I got accepted to University and was planning on working odd jobs until school started.

"One evening I was helping my mother prepare dinner. I was a bit of a mess from cooking. I had flour on my dress, was wearing no makeup, my hair was pulled straight back with a scarf tied around it, and I was in my oldest dress. There was a knock at the door. My father went to answer it. A few moments later he called out that there was someone to see me. I figured it was one of my girlfriends dropping by.

"I turned the corner into the living room from the kitchen, and there he stood—the most handsome ghost I had ever seen. Andrius had come to see me.

"Oh, Klara!" Nika said. "How wonderful!"

"He was a lot thinner than I had remembered. There was much pain in his eyes. He looked older than his age. But it was most definitely Andrius.

"I'd like to tell you we ran together immediately, like in movies, but both of us could hardly believe we were seeing each other.

We just stood there staring. After I got over the initial shock, I remember what a mess I must look like, but Andrius moved toward me with his hands outstretched. No words were spoken.

"I was thankful my dad excused himself from the room. But I knew he and my mother were peeking around the corner. They had already expressed concerns about a future husband for me. So many of our men had died in the war. They were fascinated with the fact that a nice young man was standing in our living room, wanting to see me.

"Every detail of the next moments are forever etched in my memory. Andrius reached up and moved a wisp of hair from my forehead like he couldn't believe I was real. Then he took my left hand and looked down.

"'I see no ring,' he said. 'You are not married?'

"'I am not married,' I said. 'I'm not even seeing anyone, but what are you doing here? How did you get here? They said you were attacked by four German fighters and that it was impossible for you to have survived.'

"'I will tell you all of that,' he said. 'But for now, I want you to know that the only thing that has kept me alive these months is the thought of seeing you again and maybe getting a kiss from you. May I?'

"Of course, I could not refuse such a request," Grandmother said. "I leaned in. It was a simple kiss. Nothing like you see in those movies nowadays. We were two very hurt and damaged people in a nation of hurt and damaged people, and we needed to heal.

"Once we had kissed and he finally smiled again, I felt my heart release the bitterness that I had held in it ever since I'd known of him going down while trying to fight off four German fighters; I knew we could heal together.

"'How did you survive?' I asked him, again. 'How did you find me?'

"Andrius reached into his pants pocket and then opened his hand. There it was. The piece of paper that I had written my address on. Part of the address was stained in blood.

"'Andrius!' I said. 'Is this your blood? How badly were you hurt?'

"Yes, it was his blood. Yes, his plane was shot down. At way too low of an altitude, he had been forced to bail out of the plane. He survived the impact, but his legs were broken. I can hardly imagine how he managed to do so, but with two broken legs, he was still able to crawl and elude the Nazis for three days in the forest; but they finally caught him.

"Instead of them shooting him immediately, they made him a prisoner of war. He was tortured, starved, and beaten for months. The war ended, and he was rescued by the Americans, but he required lots of medical attention and was in a hospital for a long time.

"They never could fix his legs completely, so your grandfather walked with a limp the rest of his life. He said each time they finished beating him, after they had left him alone, he would pull out my address from where he kept it hidden in his clothing. He would stare at it, at my handwriting, and escape from the pain into a dream of finding me.

"That address helped give him a reason to live. He said he became a little superstitious while he was being tormented by the Germans. He began to believe that as long as he protected that paper, he would survive and someday get out. He had imagined us meeting again over and over in his mind. Once he arrived, it was hard for him, at first, to believe it was finally true and not something he had made up.

"Now, suddenly, here he was in my living room.

"It is strange to say this, but I had not cried since the day the war had ended, when I sat at that little stream. Even my parents told me later that they could see I was just going through the motions, trying not to feel anything. Trying to go back to the eighteen-year-old I had been before the war, but it was impossible. I was not the same person. I never would be.

"Now, with Andrius standing in front of me, I started crying. I threw my arms around him and cried tears of relief and joy onto his neck while he held me. Soon, I felt his hot tears also, through the fabric of my dress. I have no idea how long we stood like that. Simply holding on to each other as though each were an oasis to the other.

"That feeling never completely went away. Andrius and I were always an oasis to one another. We knew how precious life was, and how fragile. We never wasted time by fussing at each other.

"We all stayed up the whole night talking. My mother kept feeding him, and I was glad, because he was so skinny, and I wanted him to get his healthy weight back. As we all talked and ate, the relationship and the healing grew.

"I could tell my father liked Andrius immediately. Any man who would dive into the middle of four German fighters to save his friends, endure countless beatings, and live just to see his daughter—was most worthy of his blessing. That was something Andrius asked for a few weeks later, when he told my father he would like to marry me.

"The fact that Andrius wanted to marry me wasn't a big surprise to my father, and it wasn't really necessary to ask my father's blessing. I had certainly earned the right to decide if and whom I would marry, but my father respected Andrius for keeping to tradition, and he gladly gave his permission.

"Our wedding was simple by choice and by necessity. Goods were still in short supply. Our country had given so much to the war effort that we struggled for quite a while to get back on our feet. There wasn't an abundance of anything in post-war Russia. Still, we invited all our friends. Everyone pitched in, and it was a most wonderful time. My friends from University found what flowers they could and made a few arrangements.

"Friends of my parents raided their own meager food supplies and managed to create a wedding feast. I wore my mother's old wedding dress, which was a touch too big for me since I had lost so much weight during the war. Andrius told me later he never even saw my dress, he just looked at my eyes the whole time, afraid I was a dream, a figment of his imagination. He had a deep romantic well within him.

"Andrius finished a degree in engineering. I became a teacher instead of working as a pilot. I had had enough of flying. Together we made a good team.

"Then an opportunity came up for us to move to America. Andrius was offered an excellent job. The job offered more money than he could possibly make in Russia. We were young and ready for such a challenge. We jumped at the chance. I was pregnant when we left Russia, but your father was born on American soil. We built a good life there, an enriched life. We made many friends. It felt good to make friends that we did not have to hold ourselves back from caring for too much for fear that they would disappear in flames the next day.

"And that," Grandmother said, "is the rest of the story. I was fortunate enough to marry one of the best men I had ever known. We loved each other and took care of each other. In addition to that, I have had your father, your mother, and you to love. I have had a blessed life."

"That is the most beautiful love story I have ever heard," Nika said, tears streaming down her face.

Owen even felt himself choking up. "Now I wish even more that I could have known my grandfather."

"Ah—you do not need to have seen him to know him,"

Grandmother said. "I see so much of him in you, in your heart especially. You know him by simply being who you are."

"Andrius and I met on an airfield in the middle of nowhere, but it was as though we were meant for each other. Who knows, maybe your love story will be that you met your future wife on a train, in the middle of nowhere in Russia, helping an old woman see some friends one last time?"

Nika blushed and glanced away. Grandmother had embarrassed them both, but she didn't seem to mind one bit. In fact, she gave Owen an exaggerated wink as though she had just done him a big favor.

"You are incredible, Grandmother." He didn't know whether to be upset with her or to laugh. "You are deliberately embarrassing me and Nika."

"I know," she said, happily. "And I am enjoying it very much."

THIRTY

In Owen's mind, the train ride was ending way too soon. They were about fifteen minutes from the Moscow train station. He and Nika had already traded contact information. She had said if she could get away from her family, they would try to meet up for some sightseeing.

Understandably, he wanted to spend more time with her, but he knew he was there for his grandmother. About that time, Owen's grandmother said she needed some help.

She reached deep into her travel bag and pulled out a dark blue velvet case. Her old hands caressed the top of the case for a few moments, and then she slowly opened it. Nika gasped, and Owen was shocked.

Grandmother could not help but have a small look of pride. Lying there against the blue velvet was a group of medals.

Nika asked, "May I?"

Grandmother nodded.

Nika picked up one of medals and spoke to Owen, "In one of my Russian history classes, I had to study and give an oral report on Russian medals. I never thought I actually would see these in person."

"Would you care telling me what each medal means?" he asked.

Nika pointed at one of them. "This one is the Hero of the Soviet Union medal. It is no longer awarded, but during WWII it was about the equivalent of being given the Medal of Honor in your country."

"Goodness, Grandmother," Owen said. "You certainly know how to keep a secret. The equivalent of a Medal of Honor! And you didn't tell anyone?"

His grandmother just shrugged. "They were Russian medals. I doubt anyone in America would have understood."

Nika picked up each medal, looked each one over carefully, and then handed them to Owen to admire and touch. "This medal here is the Order of Lenin; it is another medal no longer given, but up until the Hero of the Soviet Union medal was created, this was the highest medal you could receive."

Grandmother smiled at the looks of astonishment that Owen was shooting at her with the explanation of each medal.

Nika continued, "This medal is the Order of the Red Banner.

For a long time, it was considered the most prestigious medal in military circles, because it could only be awarded for combat heroism. That changed in time, but believe me, every medal your grandmother has was earned for combat-related activities and was not some political or civilian thing.

She chose another one. "This fourth medal is the Order of the Patriotic War First Class."

Grandmother said something, and Nika translated, "She just told me she got this one for landing in enemy-controlled territory, repairing her plane, rescuing a Soviet soldier, and taking off again while under fire."

All Owen could do was shake his head in wonderment.

"This next medal is the Order of the Red Star. It is a bit more of a general medal, but hers was awarded for general bravery in combat."

"What am I going to find out next, Grandmother," Owen said, "that you were once the President of Russia?"

"Stop interrupting," Nika said. "I'm not done! This next medal is for Battle Merit. It is pretty much given for what the title says."

"May I have the honor of pinning these medals on you, Mrs. Petrov," Nika asked. "Now that you are back in Russia, you must wear them."

"Thank you, Nika," Grandmother said. "Now that I am in Russia, I would like to."

A few moments after Nika got the medals pinned on, the train came to a jerking stop.

Klara stood, and they started walking out of the train. It was an amazing thing for Owen to watch. Grandmother walked taller and prouder than he had ever seen her do.

Those medals changed her, as well as the people around her. The moment she walked off the train, men and women would tip their head, put their hand over their hearts, or even salute her as she walked by. Owen stayed a few steps behind. His grandmother had earned this honor, and he didn't want to do anything to distract from it.

He turned, hoping to get one last look at Nika or maybe even get a goodbye hug, but she was already gone. He did not know if she would try to get back in contact with them before the reunion, which he had invited her to attend with him, but his grandmother had made sure she had the name of their hotel, just in case.

THIRTY-ONE

OWEN and his grandmother spent the next two days doing some sightseeing. He got to see Red Square; they tried to see where she had grown up, but that neighborhood had been replaced with office buildings.

Her old University was there, and when they stopped, there was no problem getting a little tour with those medals hanging from her coat. She showed Owen where she and Andrius would meet between classes and have lunch after they married.

She especially loved simply sitting on a bench, watching the people walk by, and telling Owen stories about what it was like living there so long ago. These conversations took a long time, and Owen cherished every moment.

The night before the reunion, they returned to the hotel early, because he wanted to make sure Grandmother had plenty of rest for her big day. There was a message from Nika on the hotel phone. She said she would meet them at the hotel lobby first thing in the morning to take them out to breakfast, and then they could go on to the reunion together.

THIRTY-TWO

TRUE TO HER WORD, Nika was in the lobby. She was so lovely, she took Owen's breath away. He had thought she was beautiful on the train, but now she had been home, gotten some rest, was wearing a pretty, yellow, spring dress, and she was stunning.

He liked how she went to greet his grandmother first. Grandmother had her hands out for a hug, and they embraced. Then they started chatting a million miles a minute. Too fast for Owen to begin to catch any of the words.

Finally, they stopped, and Owen asked, "Care to fill me in?"

Nika just laughed, "Klara was just telling me what a perfect gentleman you have been and how you haven't asked one girl for her digits since I've been gone."

"Really, Grandmother?" he said. "You want to continue to embarrass me like this?"

"I'm just an old woman. I don't know what you are talking about. English is not my first language."

Owen rolled his eyes.

They took a taxi to a small city airfield. Open-air tents had been set up. Owen and Nika helped Grandmother walk to the tents.

Other female veterans were filtering in. This was the moment Grandmother had been waiting for. She made it clear that she didn't want or need Nika and him interfering. They walked a little outside of the tent to a large tree and leaned against it while they watched.

The old women were talking to one another with great enthusiasm. Some were reenacting airplane maneuvers with their hands.

"I hope that when I'm that age I can say I did something great," Nika said, "that I did something noble. I want to be able to say that I stood up for those who could not."

"I agree," Owen said. "But you have to admit—those women are a hard act to follow."

Nika glanced at her watch.

"Do you need to go somewhere?" he asked.

"No, it's just that my father has arranged a surprise. Don't ask me about it. I'm supposed to keep it a secret—but you will like it, and so will Klara."

A few minutes later, he thought he heard planes coming in. He didn't think much about it. It was an airport after all. But he saw the women veterans stop talking, and every one of them looked up as though trying to see through the tent ceiling.

The next thing Owen knew, Nika had disappeared, and he was hearing her voice over the small speaker that had been set up. She was speaking in Russian. All the women were listening intently to Nika's speech. What could she be saying? Then all the women yelled in glee—including his own grandmother—who was standing and clapping with delight.

Nika walked back over to Owen and said, "Dad and I have been working on a surprise for the Night Witches these past couple of days. Wait until you see!"

As the women made their way out of the tent and toward the airfield, Owen watched three planes flying low over the airfield.

"Is that...?" Before he could finish, Nika completed his sentence. "Yes, those are old Po-2s. My dad sometimes has to charter planes to oilfields in the middle of nowhere, and as it turns out, some of those companies also restore and fly vintage planes for air shows. A few of those business friends of his are lovers of the old Po-2s. They are here to give rides to any of the women who might want to go back in time for a few minutes."

"Nika, I can't believe you did all this. Just listen to the delight in those women's voices! They are all so happy."

"Hey, all I did was tell my dad all about Klara. He knew about the Night Witches, and he couldn't wait to help. He should be in one of the planes coming in, as a passenger."

The three planes landed and came to a stop directly in front of the tent. The women made their way out to look at them. Some were oohing and aahing, and others looked like they were being somewhat critical of the setup. Owen figured they were probably the mechanics.

One of the pilots came over to Nika and Owen. He looked imposing with his 6-foot 6-inch frame, leather flight jacket and aviator sunglasses. But the moment he spoke, he was just as warm and friendly as Nika.

"Hi, I'm Dmitri, Nika's papa."

"Hello, I'm Owen."

"Thank you for taking such good care of my daughter while she was on that very long train ride," Dmitri said.

"Sir, it was the opposite. She took care of me and my grandmother."

Klara came and stood next to Owen. Before Owen could introduce her, Dmitri introduced himself.

"You must be Mrs. Petrov. I can see the resemblance with your grandson. It is my honor to meet you," Dmitri said, as he put his hand on his heart, tipped his head in respect, then shook her hand.

"The honor is mine. Meeting the man who has helped raise such a wonderful daughter," Klara said.

"Thank you for the compliment, but I'll give the credit to her mother, who will be disappointed that she could not be here. Her flight was delayed this morning."

"That is a shame," Klara said.

Then Dmitri spoke loudly in Russian to the crowd that was forming. "If you ladies are willing, we will begin giving all of you rides. It is the least we can do for Mother Russia's brave Night Witches!"

The pilots and airport ground staff helped the ladies take turns climbing safely into the seats behind the pilots. Flying helmets and goggles were put on and fastened, and then each plane powered into the sky. Some of the women squealed with delight. The planes were flying so low, Owen could hear them from the ground.

The only sad thing was that some of the elderly women were not physically able to go up, but their smiles were just as big, getting to sit there and watch. It took a while, but every woman who could got a short ride, and the pilots had many lipstick marks on their cheeks.

Owen heard the pilots saying the same thing over and over to each woman who thanked them for their ride.

Nika translated. "It is our honor to ride with a Night Witch. Thank you for helping save our country."

Finally, Klara took her turn. She was the last one. The others had already wandered back over to the tent. Dmitri was the pilot. Owen helped her into the cockpit, making sure her straps were tight and her goggles secure on her head. She felt so fragile to him, so little. He felt almost like she might break up there but told himself not to worry. She was most definitely tougher than she looked. He stepped back to a safe distance, and with Nika, he watched his grandma take off. They landed about ten minutes later.

After his grandmother landed, Owen asked her, "How was it?"

"Wonderful, but…"

"But what?"

Klara frowned. "Give me a few weeks, and I could turn this nice young man into a real pilot. He flew much too carefully!"

Nika's father, still in the seat in front, heard every word.

"Would you like to go up again, Mrs. Petrov?" he said. "I would love to tell my flying buddies that I had been schooled by a real Night Witch."

The last thing Owen expected was for his grandmother to accept.

"Put me in the front, Dmitri," Grandmother said. "You can take the navigator's seat."

With great misgivings, Owen helped his grandmother and Nika's father make the exchange. Even Nika looked concerned.

"Is this a good idea?" she asked.

"I don't know," her father said. "But this I do know. If a woman with those medals on her chest wants to fly the plane, she gets to fly the plane. If anything goes wrong, the navigator's seat has controls."

Of all the things Owen had ever seen in his life, the next few minutes were the strangest. His little grandmother in front, crouched over the controls, a determined look on her face. Nika's tall father in the back.

The other women came out as they saw what was happening. A small crowd gathered as Klara taxied slowly down the runway, hunched over, checking out the various controls.

Dmitri looked up at Owen and Nika and held up both hands laughing, showing he was clearly not in control.

At the end of the runway, she turned the plane around, and the next thing Owen knew, his grandmother came tearing down the runway with the plane lifting off directly in front of the crowd. He could see Grandmother clearly now, a frown of concentration on her face, and a look of excitement on Nika's father's.

The little plane climbed and climbed, people shading their eyes as they looked up in to the sky. Then there was a gasp as Grandmother put it into a steep spiral, pulling up just in the nick of time to keep from hitting the ground. Appreciative applause followed as she leveled it out and flew away into the clouds.

The plane quickly became nothing more than a speck in the sky, and then it started growing larger and larger again. It came toward the runway with a roar. Then suddenly, the roar stopped, silence reigned, and everyone held their breath as Klara allowed the plane to glide down, down—so silently that Owen could hear the wind swishing through the metal wires between the wings. The silence went on and on. Too long before she started the engine again.

Except the engine didn't start. It stuttered, and went silent, and stuttered again until all watching knew the plane was going to crash.

And then, at the last instance, the engine caught and held, and Klara and her plane and passenger soared again.

Owen heard a faint "Whee!" filtering down from the plane.

"My grandmother is crazy," Owen said, admiringly. "And all this time I never knew."

"She almost gave me a heart attack," Nika said. "But that was some good flying."

As the plane landed and taxied to a stop, Owen could hear a loud conversation going on between Dmitri and Klara.

"If this plane had been serviced by the women mechanics we had during the war, that engine would not have had difficulty starting back up," Grandmother said. "They knew our lives depended on them being absolutely meticulous."

"I'll check into it, Klara," Dmitri said.

Owen noticed that Nika's father looked a little green around the mouth as he climbed out of the plane.

Grandmother, on the other hand, seemed energized by the near miss. She took off her own goggles and helmet and shook her gray hair back. Then she unbuckled her seatbelt and started to climb out unaided, but Owen rushed to help.

"Are you okay?" he asked.

"That was so much fun," Grandmother's face lit up. "I never thought I'd get a chance like that again."

"My guess is," Owen said, "if Dmitri has anything to do with it, you won't."

When they arrived back at the tent, his grandmother was reabsorbed into the fellowship of elderly Night Witches, many of whom were patting her on the back.

THIRTY-THREE

OWEN WAS HOMESICK, but he had mixed feelings about leaving. He was beginning to care about the country his grandparents fought for, and he didn't want to leave Nika. He had finished his packing the night before. He and Nika had sat outside the hotel all night and talked until sunrise.

It was time for him to go upstairs and gather his grandma and luggage. Nika's father had fully recovered from his scare and said he wouldn't have missed his near miss for anything. He had volunteered to drive them to the Moscow airport to catch their flight back to the United States.

Right on time, Nika's father showed up. His grandmother insisted that she ride in the front seat to not get carsick. She had never complained of car sickness when they had ridden together in the U.S. He had a feeling she did that on purpose to let him and Nika sit together on the ride to the airport.

Airports are never a good place to say goodbye, no matter how the movies show it. Many people are milling about, there are security lines, etc. They had walked to where Nika and her father could not go with them past security.

There were awkward hugs and handshakes. Owen and his grandmother started to walk off, but he wanted to do just one more thing. The problem was, he didn't have the guts. Then a thought hit him. He did not come from cowards. Grandmother said she saw much of his courageous grandfather in him. Well then, he would find his courage. He sat down their carry-on luggage and said, "Grandma, please hold on for a second and watch the bags. There's something I need to do."

He ran back to Nika, took her in his arms, and kissed her exactly like he had been wanting to do from the moment he had met her.

Owen then looked at Nika's father, who was standing two feet away with a look of shock on his face.

"Sorry sir, a certain Night Witch taught me that life is short, and it is best lived with courage."

"I think she's taught quite a few of us that lesson," Dmitri said, with a smile.

Owen ran back to his grandmother, grabbed the luggage, and they got in line at the security point. His head was spinning, but he was happy.

As they waited, Klara nudged him with her elbow, "You're more like your grandfather than I realized."

"Huh?"

"Maybe I wasn't completely truthful of how delicate our kiss was in my living room that first time. Maybe I didn't want to admit that it was a whole lot more like a movie kiss. Your grandfather was a very good kisser."

"Too much information," Owen groaned. "Way too much information!"

THIRTY-FOUR

Ten years later:

It was a sad day but not unexpected. He was sitting in the front of their church, looking at a casket. Instead of flowers, there was a Russian flag draped upon it, and nearby, on a special table, Klara's medals were displayed, along with that first picture of her in the bullet-hole-laced plane that Owen had seen in her diary so long ago on that train.

The past ten years had been precious to Owen. After that trip to Moscow, his relationship with his grandmother had changed forever. She taught him to read and speak Russian. He dug into it with enthusiasm. She was so proud when he became fluent in her mother tongue. So was Nika.

Once Owen's father heard Klara's story, he and Owen went to speak to some of the members of the local Veterans of Foreign Wars, better known as the VFW. When those men and women found out that a veteran Night Witch of the Russian Air Force lived in the area, they insisted she join them.

Even though she was not an American soldier, these were mostly fellow World War II veterans, and since they were on the same side during the war, they made her an honorary member. Owen loved taking her there for social gatherings and hearing some of the old stories.

Those visits to the VFW had greatly slowed down in the past year as her health declined, as did many of her other activities. The woman who had flown through a hail of bullets passed away peacefully in her sleep.

Uplifting words were spoken, and the funeral service was soon over. Owen stood up and took his place beside his father as one of the pallbearers, while his mother and beautiful wife, Nika, looked on.

In honor of his grandmother, he was wearing his formal Air Force uniform. As he and the other five men started the long walk down the church aisle and outside into the sunlight, the sight that greeted Owen was humbling.

The men and women of the VFW were lined up. They saluted his grandmother's casket as he and the other pallbearers walked by. Even grumpy old Joe struggled out of his wheelchair and managed to stand for a moment and salute.

He knew this would be confusing to visitors in the audience, wondering why these soldiers were saluting a casket draped with a Russian flag, but Owen knew at this moment the medals and flag meant nothing. These battle-hardened veterans were not saluting a flag, they were saluting the soldier who lay at rest within the casket. They were saluting the bravest woman any of them had ever known. Klara Petrov. His precious and beloved grandmother, a Night Witch.

ALSO BY DEREK E. MILLER

An Espresso Short Series

- *Third Monkey*
- *Alien Pet*
- *Little Girl Avenged*
- *Silent Storm*

The Diary Series

- *The Attic Diary*
- *The Kamikaze Diary*
- *The Ghost Army Diary*
- *Grandma vs Hitler*

Beyond The Door Series

- *Beyond The Door Volume 1: Supernatural Anthology*
- *Beyond The Door Volume 2: Secret Societies*

Non-Fiction

- *Military Contractor's Handbook: How to get Hired… and Survive*

ABOUT THE AUTHOR

Derek E. Miller was inspired to write while being stationed in a remote outpost of Afghanistan. At the time focusing on young adult novels because of his kids, he now continues his bold and dauntless story telling with a new series, *An Espresso Short*, each containing a story that can be devoured in a single sitting while having a cup of joe.

For more information visit derekemiller.com

 facebook.com/AuthorDerekEMiller

twitter.com/derekemiller

amazon.com/author/derekemiller